Fairy Tale Paradox

Fairy Tale Paradox

by
Aashish Vatsyayan

Vij Books India Pvt Ltd
New Delhi (India)

Published by

Vij Books India Pvt Ltd
(Publishers, Distributors & Importers)
2/19 (Second Floor), Ansari Road, Darya Ganj
New Delhi - 110002
Phones: 91-11-43596460, 91-11- 65449971
Fax: 91-11-47340674
web: www.vijbooks.com
e-mail : vijbooks@rediffmail.com

ISBN: 978-93-82652-11-3

This book is dedicated to my father
Air commodore T Chand, my mother Praveen
And my sister Aastha

With special thanks to
Aishwarya for her support
And my friends
Anirudh, Bhudesh, Agneev, Aparajita and Shagun

Contents

Acceptance

As he writes the final page the man smiles, a wan long forgotten smile after many years. He had harnessed the flight for the final time and he savored the feeling, the chill running through his body his heart beating hard making him unable to even speak as the cold clasped his body, oh it was the ultimate high. He savored it and closed the book; this was all he would write. He caressed the book; it was him…in totality, a legacy he would throw out in the world for whom so ever to catch… he had done his job. The man sits for a while lost deep in thoughts and walks away never to bear claim for his work.

Neither angry nor sad the man walks and in his own way making the sacrifice that would enter him into the realm of normality, he would finally walk through the barrier and embrace his mortality. He does it with a smug grin, still knowing that he was always better than them. He walks and tides and tides of tediousness wash over him, he allows it; web grown across his wrists and feet, he allows it, moss grew over his once fast moving feet; he allows it and then he was claimed as one among many. He does not close his eyes as a final act of defiance and is smacked by the branches of the great tree, a root of which he shall soon become. He is brought down to his knees and yet he defies the great tree and stares at the stars as the great tree claims him, before he breaths his last free breath he is pacified in his thoughts that he has lit an amber in the darkest depths of the earth....he hopes he has made a difference.

The Moat

It would have been a nice warm afternoon outside, had it not been raining and she would have been fast asleep if she could get some sleep but she was wide awake, just a way of how things work out perhaps. She sat there in her castle high windows as rain poured like a little girl's tears, her tower now surrounded by a moat which would host a variety of terrible creatures but presently was flooding the garden, "should tell mom about that" she makes a mental note with a sigh she collapses on the patio and stretches, it was almost as if boredom had gained mass and pinned her down by its sheer weight and mystic powers.

"The fuck you will!!" she addresses the empty room and springs up looking outside, the rain had simmered down. The little girl had stopped crying, perhaps, just how little girls are. She ties her hair in a ponytail and decides to go out for a walk, throwing on her yellow floaters and her matching attire she steps outside inhaling the sweet smell of wet soil as she took a second to appreciate the drenched clean sight of the earth it was cold that embraced her like a police man barking at her to move along. She walks on the streets where thankfully the roads were not clogged up with water; living on a hill station had taken some getting used to. Every time she would look around all those people busy in their own chores she would smile and feel a strange sense of belonging to the place and the people.

The small hill station had a shade of gray to it; she would walk her route almost every day in the biting cold sometimes. As she would walk she would often stop at roadside book stores, for a cup of tea, some colorful hair pins, secretly buying some cigarettes which she would have with her hidden stash of rum.

Everyone had a deep dark secret she chose that this would be hers.

As she walked away she stopped at the book store, so far away from TV and other sorts of media books had become a fascination of sorts to her. Entering the shop she gave a cursory glance, which ever book would catch her fancy she would buy and devour it in a matter of days. As she hummed the tune of some song she had heard on the radio she picked up a crime thriller, not even the rum could make those bearable any more. She picked up the novel besides it, a romance novel. She always would have a soft spot for them she realized; she then made up her mind to buy 'The Scarlet Lover' a vampire romance fiction novel. There was something she found interesting about an undead vampire falling in love with a normal human being and blah blah.. blah..blah. Even the undead had a love life, much unlike her.

As she was moving to the counter her eyes fell on a small black leather covered book wedged in between some heavy books. She took it out; it had 'Fairy Tales' written on the cover in silver letters. The book was ugly and it was almost as if the author resented it so much that he had wrapped it in such a haphazard manner intentionally.

She flipped through the pages; everything inside was hand

written in pen over the paper that now was beginning to lose its sheen. There was no price tag and no author name written anywhere, this puzzled her. Megha assumed that it was one of the books handed down by people as this really wasn't a high class book store. She glanced at the shop owner sipping tea while watching the cricket match on his small TV and on impulse she stuffed the book in her rain coat pocket. It was a strange feeling that had struck Megha she had never shop lifted before and there was no reason to do so now. She moved slowly and billed 'The Scarlet Lover'. The owner without looking at her took the money and immersed himself again in the match. She left the shop behind her smiling as if she had achieved something to be applauded for. She took out the book and flipped through the pages, all hand written and in small passages, she was immediately fascinated with this strange book.

Megha returned home and locked herself in her room, it was a big house and her parents would always be busy with their own work never noticing that she was even missing.

It was night time and after dinner she locked herself in her room again, striping her clothes and wrapping herself in her blankets she took out both the books she had brought with her that day.

She took out the small ugly book. 'Fairy Tales' it read but inside there was nothing that would qualify as one, they were all "poems, so many poems". Megha tried reading some from the middle but they made no sense to her. Why would anyone write something like that and name it 'Fairy Tales' and just leave it in some random book store in a small hill station? It was almost as if the book did not belong there.

There was no continuity, neither was there any picture or

anything that would catch the fancy of anyone looking for Fairy Tales.

"Stupid book, trying to be smart with me" she said and tossed it in the pile of books she had purchased over the times. 'The Scarlet Lover' was a good read with the rum. It was so cold and the rum kept her warm and stopped the silence of the place from getting to her. Was she an alcoholic? Well no, it was a kind of relationship that had developed out of a feeling of rebellion and boredom. She was too young to worry about the consequences and too old to not do anything that her parents said was wrong, after all her father drank and he had never noticed the missing bottles from his enormous mini bar.

She continued reading the mushy vampire romance and slept reading it, there was no turbulence in the sea of life; yet.

Hidden Stash

Megha was in trouble. She sat whimpering in the back of the taxi to the airport. Almost a month ago her father had finally realized the missing bottles from the bar and had blamed the helpers for stealing from the house. It had become a big scene and then one of the helpers found the stash of rum that Megha had hidden. It rained fire and ambers for the next few days in the small house on the sleepy hill station. Her father furious had shouted at her for being so defiant of him, for allowing him to blame the help. Image was everything in a small place and corrective actions had to be taken: boarding school. Arrangements had been made for her to start her next term at St. Mary's convent for girls. It was far away from home and according to her father would bring her the discipline that she lacked so much.

After all the arrangements had been made the only thing left was the wait. The wait for the leaving date to arrive and there was dead silence in the house. Megha had become so recluse after her father had shouted at her, she would never forget his eyes and the nerves popping out as he screamed at her. Had he asked her why? Did anyone ask her why she did what she did? No, and now no one would either. Her mother sat with her and cried, she asked "why??" but it was a rhetoric question, the kind there was no right answer for.

Megha sat at the patio watching outside as it rained. She felt like joining the little girl as she cried all over the valley. Her tower, her castle, her moat, her little world of imagination and her sanctum would soon be torn away from her and the only thing she could do was wait.

She had bid her father and mother goodbye, they looked as if they wanted to say something but it was too late for that, far too late. She smiled at them and sat inside the taxi, crying almost the whole time to the airport she asked herself.

"How much farther can they push me away?"

Choices

It had been a year since Megha had joined the boarding school, the atmosphere was so different from the one she had come from but she had thrown herself into it completely to try and repress the life that she had come from. She had not gone back home once and rarely spoke at home. She knew both her parents and herself were suffering because of this but there was little she wanted to do about that.

She excelled in what they taught there, the discipline, the studies, sports everything. She would laugh and interact but there always would be a shade of gray lingering about her. In her dorm there were two more girls and both of them liked her and kept asking why she was so mellow all the time, she smiled and told them that it was how she was, it was a lie that it was.

One fine morning when Megha was rummaging through her closet after her bath, trying to find a particular shirt something fell on her foot and hit its edge against her toe. A sharp pain ran through her, annoyed she picked up the small ugly black book. She had forgotten about it in all the turmoil that had been present in her life. Still wrapped in her towel she remembered shop lifting it from the book store and a smile appeared on her face. She remembered the person she used to be and sat down on the bed flipping through the book.

She read the epilogue, something she had missed the first time she had flipped through the book, she was always so impatient then. Written in ink it read:

This book is me, essentially, the time that I have truly lived and felt alive. I have written these words as a free thinker, as an entity not as a mere human being. I leave this spark to ignite your thoughts so you may fly and no longer walk. This book is my little black heart and I leave it to you. I don't expect you to understand it, it is complicated.

The book greeted her in such a bizarre and rude way that Megha muttered "asshole", then looked around if anyone had heard her suddenly. She was alone in her room surprised at herself for breaching the things taught to her over a book. She turned the page and read the first poem captioned 'Choices'.

Choices

I have the blood of a thousand lives on my hands
It is none but my own
The thousand lives which I could have lived
The personalities I could have worn
Yet I do not lament those dreams which have bled away
Neither the times when I went astray
Nor the burden of the failures that I bear
For have killed myself a thousand times to get some clarity
For I have killed myself a thousand times to finally be...me

She read it again and again and a feeling of cold, a shiver ran through her body, she understood it. She understood what the book was talking about or maybe because it was the most pressing thing on her mind: guilt.

It's about the freedom from guilt written in simple plain English. It was what she could not understand for a year, the reason for her resentment and not going home, it was her guilt. In her inner most private thought when she re lived what had happened that night, the shock, the fear, the shame and the guilt that encapsulated it all, maybe if she wasn't such a person things would be different back home, maybe they all would be living together and no bickering no fighting, no death like silence would have plagued their home. She had not forgiven herself for her naivety.

The pages simply lay there holding the words, "freedom

from guilt" she whispered again. "I have the blood…, I have killed myself a thousand times" she sat back and let it sink in. Every decision I make a possible version of me, the other versions of me are non-existent and there is no point crying for their loss, there is only the present form present and that is the one that survived the impossible and improbable odds. The failures that have come along the way, the rejections and all the adverse situations till now have come to this moment at present. It is nothing but our choices that make us, who we are, and there is always something we can do about the things we want to accomplish, it is our choices that will pave the way for it.

She reflected on this as a tear rolled down her cheek and strange warmth filled her, she knew what she should have done long ago.

Megha sat on her bed at night. She had called her parents, her mother sounded elated and her father eager to speak to her, both her parents sounded befuddled but happy as though curtains had risen before the actors could practice their lines.

One step at a time she thought, she had forgiven them of whatever she had festered inside her and now a new start was promising.

Megha read through the book with almost affection now as she read through more poems she could see the messages between the lines, the next step from the obvious of what was written. Maybe she really wanted to see a greater hidden meaning in the small ugly book of cryptic poems, but it was something she needed at the time.

The next few days at the convent were different from all those spent before, Megha now had a spring in her step and a smile on her face. Her old imagination sprung alive again and it was almost as if she was in a new place.

She had read another poem the night before, 'My Stage' the author had called it and it had completely won Megha over. She sat in class reading the small book during class; she flipped through the pages to open the poem she had read last.

My Stage

Flow in my rhythm
Today nature
Let your winds rip the sky
Flow with me as I let go
Myself, catching your wings I fly

Let the wind whistle
And let the blowing clouds dim the lights
Take me along you
To the farthest place my eye can sight

Blow as I rage
Your voice becomes mine
I roar and shout and
Scream aloud
You thunder and growl with me
As now life flows but not time

I become more than myself
As my lament presents on natures' stage
In that moment I was as innocent as a child
Yet with the wisdom of a wise sage

As I sheath my anger
And a humbling tear rolls down my eye
So the thundering clouds cease to rumble
And in the darkness the rain drops begin to fly
I sit pensive now
Calm steady & composed

The cold wind capsules my body
Yet my melancholy withholds

My grief to anger, my anger to sorrow
My sorrows turn to slumber
The cold wind ceases, the rain stops
The clouds cease to thunder

As I open my eyes
The sun burns with grace
My sorrow and going are behind me
I stand, for the world a new face

I soak the sun and drink its light
And feel myself comeback
I roar the loin's roar
I am strong now, I see the light
I stand ready for my share of grief and more.

The poem brought a smile on her face. She could completely imagine the blowing wind screaming, the anger, how it clouds up the sky with darkness. The anger stays and then pours down as rain almost as if nature was crying with her. How the mood changes from anger to grief to tiredness and exhaustion, it reminded Megha very acutely of the first few nights she stayed at the convent. She remembered that night as it had rained she had cried and her anger then gave way to sorrow, as she had gone to sleep, it too had stopped raining and only an occasional thunder broke the silence. The next morning she had decided to put up with whatever came her way.

She always kept the book close to her, she did not know the person who wrote it but it was a friend she never had.

Names

He had been a part of the great tree for several years now. It seemed to him almost an eternity. He was walking holding the roots lest the vengeful branches should smack him down again. He had been forced to kiss the dirt so many times by them. Every time he fell he would think of his wings, the ones he cut away and he would remind himself why he did it. He would have to start again, walking at pace with the earth where high above the sun kissed the clouds and the stars shone with glee as the moon rose.

He would not think about it, a whip like sound broke the silence and he was on the ground again. The great tree swayed almost as if it were dancing with its branches covering the sun. He often looked around as people passed him by walking straight in their own set paths it seemed almost unreal how these people did not see the tree and what it did to them. There was no more fighting he was looking forward to, as he started walking again keeping his eyes set in front of him thinking of the goal ahead and nothing but.

The walkers looming around him, his body no match for them but his will was strong, even as a slave of the great tree he did not fit in, he did not belong. They called him by the name given to him…Rahul, they would call out and he would respond. That's all he was reduced to; a name.

There was still a lot to be done and he would have to live through the choices he made. He looked once again at the tree above him and was rewarded with another blow leaving him on the ground. He laughed and continued walking; he would burn the damn tree down one day if he could.

Oasis and Mirage

Megha had read the book several times over and she was in love with the cynicism, the rhymes, what it spoke to her. She would carry it everywhere it had become her personal treasure. People began complimenting her that she had changed and was so much more vivacious than before, she would smile and tell them that she felt like herself again, and she did as well.

She would try and write poems somewhat similar to the book, she wondered what the poet would say about her work.

Though she read the book many times over, there were things she could not understand, there were missing pieces that she could not bridge through. What was the metaphor behind walking? Was there even one present? What did the epilogue mean? She continued reading through the poems and found if not the meaning of the symbolism that was used she could still piece together the person who wrote the poems, there would always be strong emotions emerging in different poems. She was reflecting on the poem she read, 'Oasis', where the poet used the desert as a difficult passage of his life and the oasis as the only means of salvation or respite. It could be about love, love of a woman? A mistake he might have done? The 'Mirage' was the indicator of false pacification almost like a siren. She would imagine a person staggering through the desert and watch him wake in agony stirred so many feelings…sadness, disappointment, loneliness, hurt but all so cynically. The poet may not have written it personally maybe it was just the imagery and the contrast that brought him close to such theme. The one thing she could piece together about the poet was that he, she often imagined the poet as a he because of the writing and the grubby style of presentation, a woman would not let go of something so personal out in the open world or so she thought, the thing she could piece together about the poet was that he was aware of the feeling of loss and had felt the yearning for something that was denied to him. There was something beautiful in the sufferings of the poet as it had brought forth such amazing pieces of work.

Oasis

Staggering and alone
Walking for miles
Under the sun I burn
Gasping and dry
Yet drenched in sweat
Sand, Anywhere I turn

The desert of wanderers
The desert of deception
The journey you know not
When will end;
You know not of its inception

Fooled by mirages
Of promises of life
And tales of rivers and seas
In my desert, my desert of deception
I slept but never rested
Almost forgot to dream

Forgotten the stay in grassy meadows
As now I live
Life of no fear or attention
In the land of frost
In the land of warmth
In my sweet desert of deception

A blue jewel sparkled ahead
An oasis, with water as pure as sky
Sparkling like stars I kissed it
And sighed, the oasis took me in
Cradled me, I felt gentle breeze
As I lie.

At peace at last
His body aching of wear
Intoxicated, by life; its allure
Only when the burning earth
Wakes him he shall know
He fell in love with a mirage once more.

Confession of a Friend

As recalled by: Bhartham Reddy

(Mr Reddy was found and interviewed by Megha in later years)

He had not always been a lost cause you know; some may say that he left too early on you know. People would always say he was lost in his own world you know, true, he was; a world where he was free from the bonds and chains from futile monotonous activities you know. He knew the reason behind all this oh he did, perhaps that was his biggest problem. Sense of belonging was the first among many constraining binds and more would soon follow, he knew…you know.

He often told me that in his own sanctum he saw people as what they really were, not by their posts or relations but break them down to what others could not see or what they were hiding from the world you know, I cannot understand sometimes what he said you know.

He always was an odd little boy you know, so aware of the people around him yet so lost in his surroundings.

One time long ago when I was travelling with him in our college bus I remember him staring outside with his big eyes and looking at me asking me to look at the reflection of the building in the water you know; I casually glanced and looked away. He started scribbling on the small note book he always carried around with, a small black book.

He later showed me smirking asking me to read what he had written.

Floating House on Water

As I sat on the water edge
The mirror reflecting back my world upon me,
No matter how far I could run
I would have this reckoning

The floating house on water
The inverted life of mine
In my sanctum of illusion
In the delusional void of time

I am to exist here
For these are the choices I made
How life brought me bad cards
And how poorly I played.

From here my past
Stands tall and vast
From my mistakes
A looming shadow is cast
Which dims the light of prosperity

This is my realm of mistakes
The solid weight of the baggage I carry
My inner walls of confinement
The place where guilt and remorse did marry

The floating house on water
The inverted life of mine
Is my sanctum of illusion?

In the disillusional void of time

It was no epiphany which led me out
Scared and daring I was
I was nimble in my trout
I fell, I rose but still I drove
As I stepped outside
My head spun over

The house stood tall on ground
Only its reflection on water did shine
Which house to live, which life to live
The decision was only mine

Am I to live under the times
When my poorer decision won
And cast away my ship of free life
Whose long journey was just begun?

The house that stands is my life
The choice is purely mine
My mistakes my past
Will only reflect on me
Till the end of our time.

My past and present simultaneously persist
The house and its image; both do exist

I obviously understood nothing as asked him what it meant. He looked at me almost annoyed and said it could mean whatever I wanted it to, you know.

We never were really good friends but then he didn't have those many friends. We did have some good times though but that's all I could tell you about him.

Conspiracy

The boy remembered when he was younger, when Rahul was younger writing each and every one of those poems. He remembered the feeling he had; he could almost feel it in his skin. He would look round and everything would be so mundane, such a conformist scene he would see every time he would look around. Sadly most of the things he saw then he was a part of now. People around him grew bonds based on insecurities, dependence bonds so restrictive and primitive because everyone is afraid of being alone, well not everyone but he did not feel sad for those outcasts. His writings were the only things that kept him alive in those times, he had almost felt that to be a nobody was everybody's dream, to quietly and conveniently slip under the blanket and live a complacent and comfortable life; he had found the mere notion of something like that confusing and stupid. All those people in his past were now roots of the great tree and were living happily in the bonds that restricted them from so much. The branches were nothing more than these bonds and the roots were the promises and roles that everyone took up at one point or the other. The tree was caring at times, at times rigid and unforgiving even unfair at times but that is the way the tree was, spreading, growing, too great to fight, too great to go against.

It had become very clear to him from early on that everyone

had decided a mould for themselves and were very eager to fit into it. He wanted the freedom from exactly this, the mould made out of assumptions. May it be the one of a family man, a father, member of society? He could understand the structure and why it existed.

He was always amused at the ignorant people yelling protests at the paranoid officials, though everyone knew what was really happening they waited for some sort of confirmation from the media or someone. It was the first thing that castrated the people, this dependency on some formal declaration of the truth. How can the truth be something that someone tells you? It is a state of mind achieved when one's own mind is satisfied with the events that have taken place provided that he has complete information that is necessary. This sadly would never happen as there is dependency on receiving information and many levels before it reaches the common man. Lie to your own citizens and you can get away with anything, not the first time it would be happening in history and neither the last, hell the whole world does it. Too busy in trying to base their lives around the lies they are being told to question the legitimacy of it all. Conspiracy theories are necessary otherwise how different are we from blind men if we cannot even question what we see?

The game of survival, it always amused him. He himself now found himself in many such games. The entire dance of power, its acknowledgement and its necessity because sadly it is the way all humans are hard wired.

Dealing with people had become so much more of a concern now more than ever. It was so much easier to make characters of people and deal with them as such as all people are doomed to be scripted to be only one character their entire lives. This game of survival was full of characters one could see them walking around, talking to each other, bonding, it was hilariously transparent. The conversations were like trying to fit squares into circles so full of misunderstandings, communication gaps, so many arguments happening over practically nothing.

He saw past that, he could understand the simple art of conversation and could appreciate its intricate beauty. He wrote about it in his diary but would never reveal the trick to any one because they would think it was too stupid and because it was too simple.

It was all fairy tale lives people wanted, so completely a cliché.

Vodka

Megha sat painting her nails, in fluid sturdy motions she applied coat after coat, the bright shade of red blazed on her feet. The cosmopolitan opened besides her as her music player blazed maroon 5 into her ears. '100 ways to find if your man is cheating!', 'kissing tips to keep him craving' were the prime articles that had fallen under Megha's attention. It had been a month since she had started dating. Now in a co-ed college as she had stressed while selection perusing journalism she shared a hostel room with two other girls, presently one of them stepped into the room smiling peevishly. As she closed the door and bolted the latch the smile became an absolute evil grin as she revealed a bottle of vodka and three shot glasses. Megha hadn't drunk since the time she had been caught drinking at home but it seemed a good time to overcome that hesitance and start afresh. It was almost 12 in the night "that warden bitch won't be troubling us tonight!!" said Candy (originally Karamdeep Kaur) with a distinct pride and a hint of Punjabi accent. Anagha (originally Anagha) sat cross legged on her bed as the 3 shot glasses were placed on a make shift suitcase/ table. There was a hint of hesitation in the air; the girl's hostel had so many dimensions to it. All men wanted to be in it, all women want to be out of it. Image was everything in the hostel not just with the warden but also with other girls as well. There was always constant talk happening mostly because of boredom of other girls and boys. 'That type' was the ultimate tag which would guarantee social suicide of anyone's image. The name calling ironically was done more by the girls having more tendencies to do the same things, maybe because they were afraid that they might even enjoy it.

But none of that would happen that night as the girls looked at each other and an unsaid pact of loyalty was made. Candy picks up the glass and says "cheers to Megha's husband to be!" As both she and Anagha drank up, Megha was left red faced and muttered "bitch" then broke into laughter and drank up as well.

The laptop played the latest songs as they drank, danced and laughed. The bottle of vodka (quarter) had managed to hold its own against the 3 ladies and after a few shots neat each the bottle was winning the battle. After a couple of hours the girls had exhausted themselves and hit the bed. Anagha on the phone and Megha cleaned the place up so as to leave no proof; she had learnt her lesson long ago. Candy was passed out on the bed as Megha hit hers as well. The huge pile of clothes on the bed was relocated as she prepared to sleep. The room was spinning and she was trying to find her phone charger in her drawer. There entangled in her drawer was a black ugly leather clad note book. Megha had forgotten that she kept it there. She tossed it on the bed and put her phone on for charge. Her phone read five messages and four missed calls. They were from Rohan; she would have to call him in the morning. She opened the book thinking about Rohan and smiling a little, it was nice to be worried about. She opened one of her favourite poems.

The Puppet Show

When they met the years were young
the night was the darkness
the day was the sun
they found each other in
the midst of the madness

Little they knew in destiny's
weaves they were spun
two awkward children trying
to give a name to a friendship that had
just begun

Life is a puppet show
and so it went on....

they reached for each other
in the nubile, innocent way
they found something
and then there was nothing to despair

they promised each other
never to part
but life is a puppet show....
and every puppet has its part...

as life would have it
these young seeds did grow

their destinies led them to different locations
but the young love did withhold

so natural it was
they were a part of each other's lives
no secrets were kept admits
no space for lies

as they grew again
they found their bond had worn
their different lives served a thorn
which dug deeper
as every day did pass

to their senses they were reckoned
not them
but their time had passed....

they aged and waged
in life so engaged
so much had changed
since they had last met

all ties had been broken
and foundations shaken
to live own life
and chase future up ahead

little they knew...
their ambition had failed them
and the world had impaled them
to a hollow empty abyss

the illusion of happiness

on which one entrails
often falters and is fazed
the more you walk on it...
the more it is delayed!

But life is a puppet show
and so it went on....

one day two familiar faces
in the crowd
happened to meet
so happy they were
there was so much to speak!!

The flowers, that smile
those talks, those eyes
the safety, the warmth
those dates, the mall!
happiness.... to sum it all

things had never gone
but were back again
the young love is never lost
but is never the same

the thorns had given way
for the flowers to bloom
but is it not true
what makes any bond stronger
is gloom?
Life is a puppet show
but love a reality
no matter how complicated
we can overcome the disparity

one day as they roamed
happy and content
marveling the weave destiny had spun
in their hearts there were
still two awkward children
trying to give a name
to a friendship that had
just begun....

The poem was so different from the dark and serious poems written, it was among her favourite ones because she could see herself as this girl making mistakes in relationships and finally meeting the man she was meant to meet. But she also understood the sarcasm that he had hidden quite beautifully. People are puppets and play along to the series of events that happen and then claim to be in control of a situation when they were no more in control than a small puppet being yanked by its ropes. It could mean something more as well but before she could finish that thought she fell asleep with the book in her hand.

Morning rather afternoon would wake all of them up. She had dreamt of puppets and stages, it was all rather funny. Rohan was calling her and she greeted him with her cutest 'good morning handsome', it seemed to solve most of the problems. Somewhere in her mind the amber of sarcasm of the puppet show was glowing slowly.

She spent the whole day with Rohan and had a very good time.

It had been a good day.

Changes

The tree was a strict task master as he commanded more and more roots to bind his feet and branches to yank his hands to work, all a part of the machinery. He noticed a small triangular scar on his hand. He remembered how he had gotten the scar. It was a long time ago now he remembered how he had sat in his room with a broken heart and a quivering lip. He had let the feeling pass for but a moment. He had fallen in love with innocence; something he had lost long ago had come into his life, his thoughts. He had sworn to protect it, he thought it was the missing thing inside him that would finally make him complete and make him a better person in hind sight perhaps it had. He had fallen for the first time completely in love and all he felt now was pain…in abundance. He remembered sitting and trying to understand what had just happened and he could not understand what had just happened. He did everything correctly, not as the cynical person he was but as anyone would have and should have done. He had crawled outside his shell and found darkness waiting for him, there was no warmth; it never belonged to him.

Had he been happy then he knew he would have grown roots and perhaps would not be the angry person he was today. But he had missed his chance. He thought about that incident many times but he knew than the past and the made up future is never as good as it should be. It was the change that had guided him to this position, the change of time, the change of emotions; the change of friendships. He had never forgotten those days of confusion and vulnerability.

He remembered etching into his skin three long marks forming a triangle to escape the state he was in, it had worked, he felt no pain but the rush of the cut revived him back to his normal state.

He understood that there was no affection waiting for him and that was okay, but the sheer momentum had dragged him into a realm he did not want to be in, the saddest thing was that he fostered no resentment or hatred towards things innocence but was grateful for having felt anything at all. The happiness and the pain he kept them inside him, and had used them to push himself farther ever since that day.

That was the time he remembered he had taken his first flight, it was so glorious.

He had risen above the normal land of the walkers and risen above cutting all the roots and branches that rose to grab him, he fought his way through the attacking leaves and rose much higher than he ever had. The canopy of leaves was still high covering the sun; he flew over the land where he had suffered till now. That high above he had felt peace, tranquillity. He opened his eyes and saw everything so clearly.

He always described it as the land of earth and water. The land spreading wide across was full of walkers; people in their set pattern, in their race, walking towards their goal slowly but surely. Some ran some crawled; it was full of dust and deceit. It was very primitive but enough to keep them busy.

The ones in water free from their own weight always engulfed in a viscous bliss. Doped with desire and cradled by comfort they at some level envy what the walkers have, their dedication and purpose. Something the water bodies never needed to have.

There were the healers, the death seekers, the rulers and the snakes.

It was stripped down to the essentiality of each personality and he saw the wings flying across the sky. They were the people of the sky, thinkers, achievers more importantly the only ones who had left the safety of the ground and dared to explore the sky, with no fixed direction and no sure way to fly. Many could fall and easily go astray.

He had flown free of all his burden and only his mind moved and guided him into freedom. He had never seen the branches fall from the canopy above, it had happened too fast.

Untitled

Sometimes to stop my misery
I cause myself pain

Pure brutal and physical
It is easy big in so numb
For if I wouldn't my thoughts will drive me insane
(But that is the problem, isn't it?)
I ravage and rip my flesh
Letting my duress possess me
I stake the wound but only pain bleeds away
All despair, life erased from memory

I sit half alive and wait for
My moments of weakness to pass
Then I collect myself and slowly I stagger
Waiting for pure sunshine to drink me at last

I go through the world now
With my scar of change
I would bleed myself before I ever let
Anyone make the same dark exchange.

These three simple lines on my flesh
Mark the matter of change in life
In truth, it was my faltered vision of change
Not the tip of the knife.

Crow's Feet

Painted in a sleepy shade of grey was the small hill station where Megha in her home sat with her entire attention dedicated to one cause alone. It had gone on too long but this would finish this dance. 1, 4, 5, 3. The numbers fit and Megha's brows separated giving way to a relaxed sigh. Megha had always taken Sudoku rather seriously.

Air punching her success she looked outside the window as the clouds floated across the window almost as if you could touch them.

It had been a very different vacation from what she had imagined. She had returned home and things had been as she had left them long ago, everything was good and everyone was happy again. The family had moved on and now seemed stronger than ever.

She was flipping the pages of the ugly black book as her father exclaimed from the other room "your reading!" Megha smiled and faked an angry face towards him. Her father laughed, she could now see the crow's feet besides his eyes when he would smile, and the wrinkles on his forehead when he would frown. The years had begun taking their toll on his body. Thinking about him ageing made her strangely affectionate of him and very uneasy.

She wanted to spend more time with her parents.

She readout a poem loud to her father as he sat down next to her.

Street light

Towards light
Follow my steps
I stand alone
Alone at night

The bane of darkness
Revealer of the path
So you see ahead
Silently my battles I fight

I see just ahead of me
For I know I cannot win all
Limited by power, chained down
By life
The world stands too big
And I too small

I shall stand here
For your journey is too far
Many roads lighten,
Many too dark
Follow your heart
Do what is right

No matter how far
No matter how long

When you look back
How far you have walked
I shall be standing
Your eternal source of light

Megha finished waiting to see her father's reaction, he seemed a little confused and he said it was a nice poem. He asked if she had written it and then left her to do some chores. Megha knew what the poem was about; it was about the people who are constant in your life always edging you to go forward bearing no claim on you. She wanted to tell her father about the meaning, maybe he did not notice; maybe he did not care. She smiled and said she would tell him one day.

She had noticed a change in the writing style; it was no longer filled with anger and cynicism but based on observations and filled with metaphors and symbolisms. Was it the flight the poet wrote about? She could see the person develop in front of her eyes, a person who wanted to be more than a name or a face. 'These are the times I have truly felt alive' she understood it now that these were the instants which had made the biggest difference in his life and he chose to write about them as they shaped his dreams and his aspirations. She was happy that he had freed himself from whatever had been holding him. Still she felt she could never understand something truly if she didn't speak to the person who wrote it, but that's the beauty of art that once the artist has finished it, the work can be perceived in anyway by anyone.

'I leave this amber for you to catch fire'.

He wants the reader to think about his own position on the topic and where he stands. He hasn't written this to be free but to free others! These were not moans of self pity but powerful thoughts giving solutions to problems everyone faces, in their own way. By writing it down he has made it immortal in a way, had it not been for the smallest of the sorrows he faced he would not be the person who had written this book a cryptic aspirant of free thinking who would rather be in the shadows than pretend to preach the masses.

She did not understand why he would stop writing, why be a martyr when he could have been a messiah?

She did not understand many things and they fuelled her obsession for knowing the history of the book and the person who had written it.

Do as the Romans do

He could never forget his fall, how could he? It was as clear as it had ever been.

He remembered opening his eyes, his blood flowing hard inside he laid as he had crashed down. It was pain as he had never felt before, something deep inside had cracked as his broken wings covered his body. His heart beat in a panicked cacophony. He had fallen down naked with his wings covering him, he had failed them.

He stood up, grimacing in pain as he had begun pulling his wings off his shoulders, unimaginable pain hit him wave after wave as every part of his body protested his actions. His cold eyes and his ruthless mind set to action had ripped off his wings and now on his back glowed red scars of shame that would stay with him. He immediately had realized that there was something missing inside him now, something very important.

His flight had been short, long enough for him to see the path yet too short to finish it, he had seen the aura of his dreams. He had never regretted his flight, it had been a proof that there was a better life as he continued walking slowly, tripping, rising. He knew that the land he walked on could not hold him forever. The scars on his back ached, filling him with the absence of his wings.

He had failed them; he had failed the only thing he was sure that he wanted. The great tree had played dirty to bring him down. As long as there remained roots he could not cut; he would always be enslaved by the great tree.

The stark truth was that he had been weak and allowed himself to fall regardless of every excuse that he could come up with.

The journey had changed him, made him stronger, and made him see things clearly. He saw how people around him, the walkers were moulded from their broken dreams, their failures. Failure to achieve what they had decided to do and now were heading in the direction in front of them like puppets and they would repeat the same charade. It was layers and layers of failures that had decided even their success.

How different was he from them, not very. He ran the same races that they ran, only he could see greed sitting in the end laughing, offering a carrot and treating with a stick. There were always rewards that did not really matter yet they slaughtered each other to get them. He was in their realm now, and when in Rome...

It was all a mirage and the seven sins were the illusionists, keeping every man running. The fastest wasn't able to run long enough and the one who ran the farthest wasn't fast enough. It was all a cruel joke.

Yes, he was walking in the land of broken dreams, he would walk faster than them and farther than them all; a deep fire flickered inside him. He had not given up just yet.

Imprints

To derail from this
To answer the light
Scarred into life
And burnt into mind
The relations
The times
The way of life
Be one among many
One of a kind

Disintegrate all thoughts
Yet survive
Cut all ties
Yet you do not die
Trap yourself into illusion
The path to nothingness
Why is the world around us?
Why do we exist?

No answers no doubts
Far ahead in the rat race
Should I scream out loud?

Weak shells; to contain something stronger
Simple needs; unforgiving compromise
How to sleep; when it rages inside

To haunt for glory
To live in death
To connect to power
To pay the debt

I cry
As this body fails me
My mind betrays
Lest my soul remains hungry

Hungry for more
To know why
To derail from this
To answer the Sky

One life among many
Some choices among many
Many suns before I die
But why one more if any

Beautiful insignificance
Oh my mistress
Why play this horrid game
Of lies and shame
They will follow you
As it all ends the same

Sita

Rahul had been dreaming. In his apartment he rested in familiar settings, the old posters now having lost their glory hung on the walls reminding him of the time he always considered long lost, they were however just at arm's reach it seemed. He had moved out of his home right after finishing college and shifted into this apartment. The times he would be up to something, no good inside these walls may it be secretly drinking whisky or smoking or even watching a shade of dirty on the internet he had done it all under this roof. And now here he was, the same face, the same mind in same surroundings he wondered how similar was the boy who used to be here and the person who lay here now. He hoped nothing to be similar; the boy was weak, foolish despite all his determination to tear himself apart from his predecessors he could not help but a stray thought now and then. He reflected on his own limitations to grow and evolve and maybe he would never be able to say that "yes, I am different person now" with complete honesty. He chose to keep that part alive to remind himself of how imperfect he really was. Now, awake like many nights before he was in another familiar scenario; the sleepless nights had become sanctum of sorts for him. Things would be different now, his dreams had run him over and through but it was time to drop the mantle of assumed responsibilities towards him and the world; The Messiah? He had no answers, no solutions no clarity and this stagnation had burnt a hole inside him, how much longer could this go on. It had always been a vane struggle for significance of some sort. A new version of him was peeking to emerge and take control and the worn out lonely messiah of lost souls was more than happy to fall in the well of anonymity, where he would embrace his brother fallen before him, when he had finished his book of poems and lost it out in the open. He had put himself on the stake again and again every day and here the motions of time had brought him again, asking for his badge and gun, giving him the boot. The boy with the broken wings must sleep now in the dark wall of embracing creepers and soothing cold water, darkness to rock him to sleep. This was not why he was dreaming tonight, it was a stray thought that had not resurfaced for years now, 12 years since that boy had fallen heads over heel and the thoughts of that girl would still plague him today. He laughed at his cliché and perhaps 'plagued' would be too harsh a word for it. "Sita oh Sita", his nostalgia no longer filled with hate, anger, hurt, but a subtle reminder of the good times, it's funny how your own memories can cheat you and reset the counter of your thoughts changing the entire course of the river over a far short years. Lovely, wild, untamable, elegant and alone; beautiful Sita, he remembered the early days when he had pure devotion to her, yes devotion the type young boys have towards beautiful goddesses. In hindsight the same devotion towards her could never make her look at him as a partner, potential Rama turned permanent Ravana overnight, how graphic and vivid are those rewritten chapters of his Ramayana, it was almost funny now. Sita had penetrated his dreams, 12 years since the time he shouted in his full rage at her, he had to know what happened to her. Sleep seemed like a passenger who had missed its train tonight and would not be found suddenly he could feel a light drizzle on him and soon it began to rain and pour heavily; Rahul smiled turning he would see his sister enter the room. His sister the Rain, her presence was everywhere and strong, encompassing the view and converting the parched earth to a sweet damp land, each drop cold and alone falling down but with enough life to stir awake a rainbow. She entered and greeted him with a grand smack on his head. It was a hailstorm now with nowhere to run and Rahul could not have been happier, it continued to rain and hail through the night till morning when the thunder and lightning had their say, was pacified, they slept.

Wishing Well

There is a small
Well, hidden by growth
Just by the town walls
Where fortune is traded
By the hurt and the jaded
On the well as the coin drops

Its water had myths
Of what lies amidst
The damp stone wall
Some say it's a Djin
Or a magic fish with golden fins
Or a crystal turtle who knows it all

Wishes are poured in
Now it has filled to the brim
Its waters hide
The twirling tide
Of the dark requests within

I do not know
How many of those
Asked have come true
But I know and honest man
And perhaps his father
Had dug the well to
Quench the thirst

Of the simple man
But the well is now made of wishes of
The scared and the shrewd
I too drop a coin and wish
Perhaps
Just maybe it would
Come true.

Everywhere Rahul could see there were busy people, women bustling from here to there, men being told what to do, children either lost in their own world or just lost. The sight itself was alive and orchestrated the movements of all within it. The loud music boomed in the back ground rendering the mobile phone completely useless. He could only hope to see a familiar face in the crowd to save him from this hell. He began cursing Sita for having called him in this fix in the first place. A hand caught hold of his and he was being dragged into a side room making way through the crowd. Rahul's heart had skipped a beat as he saw Sita in her full attire pulling him close and hugging him flashing him that dazzling smile. She had if possible grown more beautiful with time. As he hugged her he felt the spat that they had was apparently forgotten with time.

"How come you didn't tell me you were getting married Verma?"

"Shut up! It's not my wedding, it's my brother's. No one has called me Verma in what 10 years now?

Things continued between them as if not a day had gone by from all those years ago, when they both were much younger and much more vane.

Sita Verma the light of the room danced and laughed with relatives and friends. Rahul looking at her from across the room noticed the way the light fell on her face. Besides Rahul were his old friends from college. He had not wanted anything to do with them. They were all good people but simple walkers and they reminded him too much of his days in college, his entire struggle with writing poems and then having to stop. He had never told them the reason he had stopped, it was because what he wrote was not expected out of him. What was expected out of him? Good grades, good image, everything that did not matter to Rahul, and it was said to be for his own good. Guilt and his own self destructive tendencies had stopped him, and in his own twisted way he had somehow made peace with that.

Only one person had been on good terms with him since those times, Bhartham Reddy, he had always called him an ape.

The wedding scene was an invasion of colors and noises to Rahul's senses. Sita now being dragged away by a group of girls looked at him from across the room flashing him her stunning smile. The ape was dancing away with his wife and drinking heavily, her name was Vineeta and she was as charming as she was pretty, he had always felt happy for both of them.

Rahul presently made his way to the roof; there was only so much of wedding he could bear. There he opened a pack of cigarettes and inverted the virgin one, something the ape had taught him in college amongst other set of unwritten rules which Rahul was suspicious that no one else followed, however this one had stuck on.

He found a nice spot overlooking the fields beyond the

building and was smoking his second when Sita entered the roof preceded by her fragrance.

"I knew I'd find you here."

"I didn't think you would leave the party."

"Yeah, all that dancing made me too hot" she said fanning her bosom. Sita had from early on mastered the trick of being seductively cute. She would have been horrible if she tried doing it intentionally but when she wasn't trying it always managed to do the trick.

She had hurt him long ago, but he no longer cared for that, he had been unhappy enough over it.

"Can I have a fag?"

"Aren't you dating one?" smirked Rahul.

"Still a jerk huh?" she smiled.

"You just bring that out in me" he replied cheekily.

"So Verma, all this time, what have you been up to, not like we have spoken in between."

"Oh! Well you know, the usual stuff...food, sleep, poop, sleep, work."

She was just one of those people who said things like that and you could not blame them.

"What about you Rahul?

"Oh you know the usual, sex, drugs, rock and roll" he said lighting a cigarette for effect. Sita laughed mimicking what he had said and they spoke for a long time catching up, insulting each other.

As the music down below stopped for a while Sita looked at Rahul and said "I missed you", he smiled back and said "I missed you too". The music roared again and the moment was over. There was no more the floral tingling in her voice, she was back to the friend he had known.

"Aren't they missing you down stairs?"

"You bored of me already? I will go then."

"Sita, before you go…"

"Yes, Rahul?"

"Answer me one thing."

"Yes?"

A tense moment passed between them.

"Where is the bathroom?"

Fall of the Ancient

Down below in a room untainted by celebration was an ancient staggering in her walk and finally fell to the earth.

Flocks of people had gathered around her attempting to revive her but with little effect. It was Sita's aunt, she was lying on the bed as children and adults gathered around her, the other ancients were busy in trying to revive her and the rest huddled in a corner keeping council. Rahul found Sita in the crowd and held her hand as she began crying. The ancients checked her pulse, her breathing, moving indecisively from here to there. There was no space for logic and reason in marriages, only magic that could somehow revive her.

Rahul left her hand and moved to the front of the crowd. He checked the pulse and then took a torch and flashed it in her eyes. There was no change in the blank orbs that stared back towards him.

"She is dead" he said to the ancients who nodded back at him and then cleared the room to perform the necessary actions.

Sita was crying on Rahul's shoulder. What had happened was as unexpected as a hail storm in summer yet had happened. Rahul saw that he was not the only one unfazed by death. The ancients having had seen more than their share of it were composed and steady in their actions. The others, their descendants were equally unfazed or in too much shock to display any sort of emotion. He could see it was the ancients who had felt the grief despite their composure; the descendants were in mere shock of having witnessed death. There was a crucial piece of humanity that had skipped them. Sita on the other hand was crying her heart out; he could almost feel her sorrow even if he could not understand it. He had always thought that her mere proximity had made him feel more human than ever. He pulled her closer as she cried into him, outside the crowd grew thinner and eventually faded away. He and Sita were sitting in a small room for a long time without having said a word.

Midnight talks

It was around midnight that Sita woke up and saw Rahul sitting near the window.

"Don't you ever sleep?"

"You were mumbling in your sleep, too funny to miss. Go back to sleep" he said smiling.

"Rahul"

"Yeah"

"I miss you."

"I am right here."

"I know and I miss you."

She hugged him as they stood near the window with the moon light falling on them. She felt warm against him, it was neither romantic nor platonic, it was strange but it felt good.

He remembered numerous occasions in which both of them had been this close, all those years ago and he had never let any feelings come into the way of their friendship. He could not taint her with anything indecent, she was perfection and he was in love with her. That was years ago, he no longer had that leash around his neck; he lifted her face and kissed her on the lips, something he should have done years ago.

She took in a sharp breath as he kissed her but then she kissed him back, pulling him closer to her. It felt as if the passion and intimacy had been overdue. He knew her like the back of his hand and as he grabbed her hair to kiss her harder it felt so right. The image of the dead woman's eyes flashed into his head all of a sudden and he pulled back, maybe he should not, there were ideals and principles….she leaned in closer and kissed him, wrapping her arms around him and he complied, he spiraled into bliss.

It was early morning and both Rahul and Sita sat under the window.

"You are dating that chap" he said.

"Yes"

"Then what are you doing here?"

"I do not know" she said. "Why did you come back Rahul?"

"Because I had to know"

"What?"

"If I was right"

"About what"

"If you were happy"

"I am."

"Have you ever kissed him like you kissed me?"

"I …I am happy you know."

"I really hope you are."

"Why did we stop that night Rahul, all those years ago?"

"You weren't mine, it wasn't right."

"You are one in a million you know that?"

"And that wasn't enough for you?" he asked her, looking away. "You broke my heart."

"You were never...just...how can I tell you."

"I don't blame you Sita; you have all the right to be happy. I would be the last person to get in the way of that."

"Did you really love me?"

"Yes"

"Why didn't you say so?"

"Did you not know?"

"Do you love me now?"

"No"

"Is that why we stopped last night?"

"I still love you enough not to make you an adulterous, it's important to me."

"I have to go."

"I know."

It was morning now. As Rahul freshened up and moved to the roof to get some fresh air he thought about last night. He did not want to stop, but for Sita's sake he had. He wanted her to be happy and he too had a self-image of a good guy that had stopped him. He understood the hypocrisy of this. His every action and hers had suggested what was to happen, yet he went against it.

He looked across the fields and could see smoke coming from a distance. There was a pyre and people gathered around it. He remembered last night's incident. It was the pyre of 'Sita's aunt. He looked at it again and made his way down. The house was alight with activity again. It did not look like a house which death had touched merely hours ago, but it no longer looked like a house holding a marriage either.

Rahul left the house and made his way through the fields towards the pyre. The cold morning air filled his lungs and he grew breathless reaching the place. He stood away from the group, the group of ancients that stood there, it was too intimate for him to breach into. He saw them standing and mourning as flames licked the body. He knew that the ancients understood that the body has passed away and it was something beyond their control. As he walked back to the house the ancients stayed there mourning the dead. He reflected on the biggest strength of human beings, the ability to feel loss; to feel loss and carry on with their lives. There was something very beautiful in those moments of grief, Rahul cringed that he could not feel the absence, he longed for it, the feeling of loss, the feeling of attachment.

Back in the house the preparations for the grand ceremony had begun. There was a stark difference between the ancients and their descendants. They both had their roles to play; one to mourn the death and the other to celebrate life.

Rahul spent time with the ape and his wife reminiscing and contributing to the celebrations. Sita had been absent from the scene all day.

The final countdown had begun all lights on, the groom and bride completely decked up were put on the pedestal. Rahul could only imagine how they must be feeling, like deer caught in the head lights of a moving car perhaps. He separated himself from the scene and came to a small empty room. The moon outside was beautifully radiant and he perched himself on a window sill.

"Rahul"

Rahul almost fell off the window as Sita stepped from into the room.

"Why aren't you out there?" he asked her.

"It's my cousin brother, we aren't that close. Have you seen Bhartham? His wife is looking for him."

No one ever knew where he ever was, Rahul remembered from his college days "Yeah, let me call him."

"Battery is dead, got a charger?"

"Yeah, I think it's in the other room."

Rahul followed her silently as some where the ceremony had initiated, with all the incantations and prayers. Almost like foreplay.

They waited for the phone to switch on in the empty room.

"I wanted to thank you, for being such a..."

"Impotent chicken?"

"Such a gentle man and not taken advantage of the situation" she finished.

"Don't worry about it."

"Had it been any other guy..."

"Had it been any other guy, things would not have gotten to that to begin with" he said

"You always confuse me..." she said

"I have changed you know, I want to be normal"

He knew even if he said something as vague as that Sita would understand despite all the time.

"You can be whomever you want, you know that Rahul"

"I want to be only one person now"

"And that will make you happy?"

"I was never happy Sita..."

"Don't change Rahul; the world needs people like you"

"People like me? There are plenty of nut cases like me! The world needs more people like you fool! People who can feel not just for themselves but for others as well..."

"I am happy you know, with him, in my little life," Sita said.

"That's what you wanted; you sold your self to being mediocre just so that you may be happy. I never understood why you did it" he spoke.

Rahul sighed; both of them fell silent for some time.

"Verma...Sita this is the last time I am meeting you. For some time at least."

"I know" she said latching the door.

"I am happy" she said.

Outside the commotion carried on with the ceremony now raging full on as inside both of them caved into their animalistic side.

It was intense, passionate and overdue; their intimacy of all those years throttled them and left all inhibitions aside and ravaged each other. It was everything both of them had known it would be. Right until they were spent, right until...

'Swa Ha!!!'

The morning light fell kindly on gloriously naked Sita as she got ready; Rahul too was preparing to leave.

"I am leaving" she said when he was fully clothed, Sita adjusting her jewellery in the mirror.

"You were right, you know. I choose to be happy, in hind sight that may have been a short sighted decision. There were things I could have done if I had to, but there was never any need to. I am happy Rahul. I see you, still alone like a wild wolf roaming through life, I know you must feel lonely at times but you have made it this far. Everyone does not have the mettle to make a difference, you were always different, and that's why you always confuse me. You would never take the easy way out. It's something I admired about you, it's stupid but I like it."

In that moment Rahul could see the girl he once knew, it was good to know she was still alive.

"Don't you write anymore? I used to adore all your poems."

"Not any more, much has changed since then."

"Remember what I said Rahul."

"There is yet hope for you" smirked Rahul as he hugged her good bye.

"And don't come back here" she said "because something like this could happen again" smacking his bottom.

"Shame, you have given up on it Verma?"

"What can I say Rahul, you just bring that out in me.

Bingo

Megha had searched tirelessly looking at every possible lead that could guide her to the author of the book, she had searched the internet for every poem caption, every word of it and found no match. It was frustrating as her obsession drove her into it more and more. This person was almost like a ghost, why so hell bent on being secretive? Why be a martyr?

'Rohan calling'

She snapped back into everyday world "hey" she answered "come out of that damn hostel!! We are all going to party at 'The Blitz' it's been ages since you've hung around with us."

It had been almost that long that she had broken up with Rohan. He could sense her pushing him away and she did not want to hurt him, he wanted everything to be normal, he wanted good things for her, he wanted to marry her. Megha had told him, he was perfect, for some other very lucky girl. It was one of the things that just go through ones heart on hearing. She was in no terms ready for marriage. She felt like a child from the inside, a child that needed its freedom.

She politely refused and received a rather rude reply. Rohan wasn't the only one making efforts with no results. It was nothing more than a formality to her now.

She sat gazing at the screen blankly again, there had to be something that could bring her closer to the identity of the person.

Looking around at her now empty hostel room she was sure of one thing, now in her final year she had done some seriously crazy parties, passed out, laughed till she cried, snuck outside, she definitely had more stories than education to take away with her.

Her family had shifted outside the hill station for some time now leaving the house for another home. She felt a little alone as her castle, her moat were now gone forever. She missed the place and its quiet peaceful environment. She had found the book that changed her life there. She opened the poem that she knew would make her feel better.

Gypsy Lives

I live a gypsy life
Travelling here and there
I leave my house for another home
Leaving just land bare

I travel far, along my way
I leave just a shadow behind
The place still stays hidden
 Imprinted in the back of my mind

One day I stood
 In the place of past
Bitter happiness, a part of me sunk
I sipped my past, its smell
Its taste, the intoxication got me drunk

A mischievous smile
Crept up my lips
With life my eyes did shine
For I was a boy a man no more
As if I had slipped back in time

I lived again the years
As I walked
As I walked down memory lane
All seemed smaller the essence of it lost

It stood waiting and plane
Ghosts I saw
I saw myself
The place where I had
Run to pick the ball
But there were no children
There were no cries
No goal, just the simple wall

I drank the essence
Of the life I had left behind
And I saw it, standing alone,
Weeds growing, windows hanging
The falling structure I had called home
Smiling sadly I enter the room
My room now shy from its days of glory
I move around and find my mark
And the place my father would often tell me a story
I think of my mates
A happy joyous tone
Nostalgia rushes past me I stand there feeling alone

I head back again
Laughing at my old caught lies
Never forgetting what I saw
Back to my gypsy life

She found solace in the words, that someone had been in a similar situation and had come through. She no longer felt alone, the book had grown older with her. The cover was wearing and the binding was becoming weak. Megha was treated better by time. She was now a beautiful woman who turned heads and carried herself with an enviable manner.

She was running her fingers over the book's cover when she found the cover had become loose from the leather covering. Megha gently removed the leather cover and lovingly began to fix it so that it is as good as new. It was then that she found a name scribbled on the book. The name had been under the leather all along!

She jumped up and danced on the bed, doing a small little gig. She bounced down from the bed and searched the name written on the cover; Rahul Veid.

The internet yielded the results in a painfully slow manner. The page loaded with results to the name Rahul Veid. This would be the time when she would be able to see the person who had become her personal hero, her guide through thick and thin. She could now finally meet him and ask him about everything he wrote, why he wrote it. She was bursting with questions and her breath could barely stay inside her as she saw the face behind the name. There were many Rahuls on the internet, as she impatiently flipped through different entries she found the mention of one of the poems in the book linked to a profile, she clicked on the link as profile loaded the information. This would be it. The photo and details loaded, it was a skinny boy with short black hair and big eyes.

She REALLY was expecting some one MUCH older; she was confused as she checked again and again. It was the correct profile, but this did not make any sense. There had been no activity in the profile for a long time now. She sent a mail addressed to him "I have read your poems; I want to speak to you please reply back."

She noted down all the information she could find on the profile, she had to meet this person now if more than ever.

Happy Birthday!

Rahul sat on his laptop, working. That's all he did anymore ever since he had returned from meeting Sita he wanted to throw himself into his work more than ever. He smiled at his co-workers as they left him, the last person working in the office. Belonging was nothing more than a clever trick he had realized. He would observe people from a distance and donned a mask every day as he got up. The mask of plain deception, it was surprising how little, people needed to connect with each other as long as you kept telling them what they wanted to hear. How little they wanted to know about you and how much they wanted to tell about themselves. There were people whose entire image depended on people's reactions to what they did. He had tried to stay polite to them; there was no need to cause them harm though he could see so transparently through their antics. He wondered if everyone could. It would be much more twisted then.

Everyone wore a mask for the same reason that he did, to fit in.

He often looked around and saw people weighing themselves as superior and inferior by imaginary markers for their self-esteem, clearly that were where evolution was headed when it separated us from monkeys. To again estimate ourselves on the size of our bananas; how accurate.

Trivial things of no firm grounding seemed to trigger the greatest bonding amongst people. They have seemed to forgotten their insignificance and have created a world in which all trivial things control their actions, almost as if they have shrunk the universe to what is relevant to them. He looked at them with such amusement as they were the ones who were stupid and happy and he was sad. Maybe he was the one who was stupid.

What right did he have to interfere in their private universe and disrupt the harmony? Ignorance is a bliss and he could see it, he laughed and returned to his work, he could just not convince his small black heart to think other than the flight which it so bitterly ached for.

He received an email from some girl named Megha saying that she had read his poems and wanted to speak to him. He stared at the screen, his entire attention focused at the email.

Who was this girl? What poems did she read? He had removed everything from the internet and there were no hardcopies anymore…except for one…the diary.

He wanted to be sure what the girl had read before doing anything about it, could be some crazy stray message as well.

He replied asking her to name her favorite ones. He would know what she had read and if she had the book, it was almost impossible that someone had found him. He smiled as he sent the mail. This was going to be interesting.

Megha was freaking out. She had been blind folded, thrown in a car and now was surrounded in a room full of people.

"HAPPY BIRTHDAY!!!!" people shouted together and Megha was overwhelmed as the cake riddled with candles was brought to her. Her heart raced, she had almost thought she was being kidnapped. Anagha and Dhruv both nursed their arms full of scratches she had inflicted, what she could do. She was scrappy.

After the entire conundrum was over with the cake and the photos she sat down on the sofa. It was Rohan's flat she had been dragged to. He came and sat down next to her "it was your idea wasn't it!" she said punching his arm. He laughed and defended himself "you were so shit scared" he laughed. "And you may look like a tiny girl but you punch like a man" he added rubbing his arm.

All the tension to find the person behind the book had finally left her in the room, a little tipsy and so truly happy. She looked at Rohan sitting beside her and thanked him for the party hugging him lightly. "Bah anything for you, more over a party was overdue" he said. She could feel the old chemistry between both of them and almost by instinct she rested her head on his shoulder, it was a nice feeling. She had missed a little support for some time now. She had been rude to him, ignored him but all the distance between them did not matter anymore. They still wanted good things for each other just that a few things had changed.

Megha almost slipped into a sleep on his shoulder. Rohan realized that and took her to the bedroom. He covered her with blankets and looked at her sleeping a little while. His heart was in his throat, she looked so pretty sleeping. A pulling sadness formed a lump in his throat realizing that she did not feel the same way about him. He closed the door and moved to the next room.

He had been having difficulties in finding a balance in his feelings towards her. He knew he had come across too strong and scared her away. It wasn't that he wanted to marry her tomorrow; just that he did not want to lose her.

Megha's bag was on the sofa and a small book poked out of it. It must be the same book Megha had been obsessed with. It was all she spoke about anymore.

There were poems written inside. Rohan went inside an empty room to see it properly. He opened the book and found one page captioned: Rum.

Rum

To the waves of the ocean
To the rays of the sun
To the ones who are with others
To the ones that are with none

Dance and swing
Drink life; but think
O passenger of sparks and fires
Of the frost and the question within
For one has too many
But what are those to others?
Live your way
Love your family, love your brother

As the cryptic
And about the plain
Is love and life spent?
In wait or in vain

Never alone
Yet with no others
Gods speak through them
Forbidden and alone...the trotter

The many
Are they your brothers?
Is the verdict pending?

Or is court adjourned
Why does silence ring the ears?
Are you swinging in life?
Or dancing at home alone

The music in the back ground played on, Rohan sat there feeling cold, he frowned and he could not understand how he felt. It was unreal. What were the chances that he would open that particular page and he was no poet, had he really understood what it meant?

He quietly kept the book inside the bag and sat thinking. The book really was strange.

Beep beep. Beep beep!! Megha's phone chirped and she got up groggy and a little started, she had never been to Rohan's bedroom before and had little memory of how she got there. She squinted her eyes and checked the time 'email received' her phone read. It was too early in the afternoon to be receiving e mails. She walked outside and there was Dhruv passed out drooling on the sofa and Rohan banging vessels in the kitchen apparently. "Can you please not break the kitchen?" Megha said tying up her hair and saw him raising cups of coffee smirking. Megha grabbed the mug and sat on the counter." you passed out" he told her, Megha remembered instantly the comfort from last night.

"Then I tried carrying you to the bed room, well that wasn't easy either" he finished smiling. Megha gave him a dirty look and laughed despite herself. Her phone chirped a reminder again for the email received and in exasperation she looked at the message received. It read "name me your favorite ones", it was from Rahul.

He replied back!!!! Megha jumped and screamed to Rohan, her eyes wide and tinkling with excitement. She had mailed him months ago, since then she had tried his phone number, address but it was all invalid. She sat down shivering mildly. Which ones were her favorites? How many should she type? She thought and flipped through the book to see the ones that were her favorite. She typed:

"The Puppet Show, the Wearing Wall, a Walk in the Rain and Oasis"

And she sent the mail wondering if she should have explained why she liked them and how she had found the book, she wanted to say everything but there may be a better time for it.

She left the kitchen to freshen up; the sudden unexpected email had woken her up completely. Dhruv had fallen off the couch in all the commotion and when no one explained it to him he curled up and slept off again. Rohan himself had a very faint idea of what was happening, but whatever it was it meant a lot to Megha. He thought of the poem he had read last night, even he wanted to meet a person who could write like that.

Megha hurried back as her phone beeped again, she had received another mail.

J Spy

He looked at his laptop with a certain amount of disdain. It was a root that had grown on him; he had become dependent on it. The screen showed that the girl had replied back to his question.

"She liked the 'Puppet Show', expected . . . Hmmm....a 'Walk in the Rain' and Oasis"

He stared at the titles for some time; he knew them all by heart and tried to form an image of this girl. What was common in all of them that could tell him something about her? Rahul laughed at the coincidence of someone having found the book, he had not expected it. He suddenly felt more alive than he had in a long time.

He was so curious about her reactions to the poems, if she had understood them; he would have to see her to decipher all of that.

"When and where do you want to meet?"

He emailed back. All inquisitions and question will have to wait for face to face.

The girl had sent the mail long back, he had apparently missed it. It was around the time he had come back from Sita's brother's wedding.

He waited patiently to see her response, she had his attention.

"He wants to meet!!!!!"

Megha stared at the message stunned and sat down on the sofa completely overwhelmed. Was it really happening? Was this really the person who wrote the book? Was he really going to meet her? This had to be her best birthday ever.

She asked if it would be okay to meet at a coffee shop near her house in the weekend.

She had no idea where he lived, where he worked, she would travel as much as required to meet this person.

"Okay, I will meet you then, in the evening around 5;" came back the reply.

Megha was jumping up and down and Dhruv fell off the sofa again, mumbling and going to the bed room now.

She was on cloud 9, she hadn't told everyone about the book but she had told Rohan about it and asked him if he would come along with her to meet this person.

"Anything for you" he said smiling and returned to drinking his coffee.

Megha sat awake, reading the book again and again. She tried matching the dots, what would have happened. She had almost deciphered all of them by now and wrote down the prominent emotions that emerged from them. Nothing would explain why he stopped writing; nothing to give her more insight into his head.

She read the last poem over and over; it was a request, a plea. It was about how a fighter begs not to be taken to comfort as he still has to fight. It hit Megha suddenly. "He wanted who ever found this book to find him! And urge him to not take the comfortable stance! That was the plea!!"

How far ahead had he thought about it? She was only just catching up now.

A Fighter's Plea

Don't let me be
Don't let me lay
Let me live in a turbulent calm
In my placid lie.
The land of plays
Not the one to indulge for me
For I know the truth
The reality I cannot make them see.
The fight for reason
The fight for self
They ask for fight
But the levels change
To fight for living
A tougher fight on its own
Yet, they fight the battle of vain
The fighter is weary
With happiness at par
He can see himself in
Levels changing
Yet he sits there
Caught in a different war.
The tired fighter
Asking let him not rest
He is yet to walk a hundred miles.
He will rest;
When he dies
When the zest

Leaves his eyes
When his heart
Cannot conjure a beat
When his eyes
Cannot guide his feet.
The fighter pleas
Not to die
There still lingers
A fire in his eye
Rest, refrain; never retain
For his home is in the sky

He lay in his bed, eyes wide open staring at the ceiling, awake. He was wondering to himself "what have I done?" His understanding of everything was in his own unique way. He had made his flight a long time back and now among the walkers, he was one of them. What would he tell her? The problem; that's all he could make her aware of, he had no solutions.

At best he could explain to her about the poems and the stories that led to them, or he would lie about everything if he found her unworthy of sharing his life. The fire still blazed inside him deeply, reminding him of the scars on his back. He was harder on himself than anyone else. A failure is nothing more than that. He was given the opportunity to do what he wanted to and he had sabotaged it himself. The roots were nothing more than his weaknesses and were firmer now than ever. He looked at his hands; they had grown harder, his body older from the time he had written that book.

He had written the book, compiling everything he had written soon after his fall. It was his way of preserving whatever he had left and now it was back. It took about 8 years for it to find him again.

He would have to travel a little to meet this girl but it was okay. He didn't mind and after all he was more curious to meet her than she could imagine.

Outside he gazed at the stars; they were mere spectators to his anguish. The stars far away were fighting against the darkness on their own, dying slowly as they did so. Even they were insignificant

He would not lie to the girl but answer her in complete honesty, if she deserved it that is.

He closed his eyes to sleep, the wise stars overlooking him, moonlight spilling from the window and the darkness cradled him slowly to sleep; his body asleep, his soul awake.

Rahul traveled and made his way to the small coffee place Megha had suggested and searched for an empty table, he checked his watch it was 5 pm now. He looked around and saw a girl sitting on the table in the end near the window. He had recognized her, her profile pictures he had seen. She looked nervous as she kept clenching her hands. He made his way to the table as she saw him and her eyes followed him to the table.

"Hi, I am Rahul."

He greeted her.

"Megha" she smiled back shaking his hand.

She was caught by surprise as she was nervous and did not know what to expect. He looked nothing like his profile photos; obviously they had been very old. She was almost expecting the skinny boy to show up, but he was different. His hair much shorter, his built more athletic, a slight muzzle and his hands were so warm when she shook them. The big eyes were the same and she looked into them.

"You look different, from your pictures" she said.

He thought about what she was saying for a moment and then burst out laughing," that was from a very long time ago, I haven't used that account for a long time now; just kept it alive till now."

There was an air of comfort with the girl, he thought, almost effortless as they continued talking; she was smart and bright, to the point. She spoke about how she found the book, how she didn't understand the writings, how she came to appreciate his works, almost as if someone had made it up. He sat there being charming and listening to what she was saying, his heart beating fast knowing where the conversation leads to; to her interpretation of the poems and their understanding. She, she understands everything? She had his attention.

Megha found him very different form what she had imagined, he was funny, so calm, a good listener ,very warm and so humane, she had expected someone right from the pages of the book deep, dark, cryptic, arrogant, but there he sat. She spoke about her life, about the book, how it had been there in her darkest of times, and how a bizarre luck she had found him, most of all that she was actually meeting him! She was a fan of his work, true, but she could not trace the words to his face, she could not imagine this man to be that, dark or detached, she was blabbering, she knew it, she understood how it would go, she wanted to tell him about the prologue, the gist of everything, she knew behind those big eyes he was waiting impatiently to know, it was amazing how he did not spare any courtesy or miss a compliment or a joke, the impatience , the hunger in his eyes she could understand, she had read about his rise and fall, but she wanted to know about the man behind it.

Shell

Let me go back to my shell
The place where I am safe
Let me crawl back to comfort
Away from all this hurt and chase.

I came out not for me
But for others' sake
I left my feet from the ground
But as I crash back
& head for my labyrinth
It only seems, pale, cold & round

Cold & empty as a palace of ice
When I went away & walked with others
My safe land is lost from me
I am washed with the anguish as are lost lovers

No more is it happy and no more is it warm
I came back to see my shell so empty
Solitude turned to loneliness & peace to silence
What stood now was my shell, but sad, lonely,
Empty ...... the one not in my memory.

I cannot go back to my shell
& with the world I do not wish to fly
All I wanted was a patch of warmth
Where when weary I could lie.

I broke free from my shell
I stand watching a new dawn
My mind is ready, my path is set
Indestructible... till I am gone.

Megha laughed "how do you know he is with me" she asked testing him.

"He keeps looking at this table."

"Maybe he thinks I am cute."

"He, must otherwise he would not have come along."

"Are you saying I am not cute?"

"I am just saying smart girls don't come to meet strangers alone. Also he isn't looking at you, he is looking at me."

"Maybe he thinks you are cute then", Megha laughed.

Rahul laughed, the moment was light and a perfect time to ease into the questions Rahul was interested in finding the answers.

"So, tell me Megha, why are you doing this alone?"

"Who said I am doing this alone?"

"You are sitting here, expecting me to have answers. Most people would have left it at reading."

"Maybe I just wanted to know why you wrote them," Megha suddenly did not like him, from inside the charming exterior the cold indifferent interior had begun crawling out; she knew this before she had come.

"What use is that, for whatever reason I wrote them. You came here for answers so ask the right questions."

"Will you answer them?"

"Yes"

"Why the prologue? Have you written more poems?"

"Most books have prologue, but that is the most honest thing I could have written, can I see the book?" he reached out his hand, confident enough that she would have brought it with her.

Grudgingly she handed him the book and he read the first few pages, smiling.

"I have been really honest in what I wanted to say. I did want the reader to explore the boundaries of being normal. Catching fire, wings all the symbolism points to free thinking. Yes, I have written more poems, the best ones aren't even in this book" he said tossing it back to Megha.

"Why??"

"They weren't needed in there" he said shrugging.

"Why do you say you have a little black heart?"

"Well, it can't feel anything. It's almost as if it's numbed now, no empathy, no apathy. I did not think it was normal. Hence the imagery."

Rahul went on to explaining the intricacies of small things which Megha felt that she had ham handedly overlooked. He spoke about many things but nothing personal.

She let him finish, just observing him and the fluidity with which he spoke about things.

"Explain the tree."

"Well, there are pockets of comfort you can live in life and there is always an option to step out of these pockets and take charge of your life, do something different. The tree is what keeps you trapped in the obvious and the crass by luring you with comfort and familiarity. It is essentially your need to conform to make sense of things. The tree is society and it will bind you to reality, to its simple difficulties. Why the oxymoron; because nothing in life is simple if you look into it too long. That's it."

"And finally why did you stop writing?"

"I could not match up to the ideals I believe in and here I am..." he finished looking sad. But he looked up and continued "if you want to know more Megha, I can help you ask the right questions, the answers will be yours to find."

Pieces of Paper

Megha was walking back, her umbrella fighting the rain and dancing with the wind threatened to leave her side. She walked through puddles of water soaking her to her feet. It was almost dark now as she reached the door. It had been almost a year since she had met Rahul in that coffee house. So much had changed since then.

She was completely drenched despite the umbrella. The wind had been so strong. Her pony tail clung on to the back of her neck she checked the pockets of her shorts for the keys. Her shorts clung on to her making it difficult for her to find anything. It was cold outside and her fingers were almost numb.

The black thread tied on her left ankle was clinging closely to her skin, her clothes completely drenched she walked inside the house and it greeted her warmly. She sighed as she kept the umbrella and rubbing her hands moved towards the room. It was pretty dark inside the house as well; she removed her clothes trying to find a towel to dry herself. She hurriedly wrapped herself in the towel searching for something to wear.

Rahul sat in the corner smoking a cigarette. Megha gasped as she turned around.

"How long have you been here?"

"Long enough."

Megha laughed "so not a gentle man Mr. Rahul Veid, exploiting poor little girls" she said pouting.

Rahul laughed "nothing little from where I am sitting."

Megha hissed at him, throwing stuff from the closet at him laughing.

Rahul had invited her to his house in the hills, so reminiscent of her own old house but a different place all together. She had come to write an article about the animal shelter, the biggest in the country for her professor. Rahul had told her he had planned to take some time off any way and after all arrangements were made he had driven them to the small beautiful little place in the hills.

She had left to get dinner for them as Rahul was painting in the afternoon, she wanted to treat him, pamper him a little in turn for his hospitability and because she wanted to. Rahul and she had grown close over the year they had known each other; she had known him for much longer by reading into his intriguing mind through his book. He was alone and she had fallen for him right from the coffee shop, he was everything she had imagined and more perhaps.

As she threw a big book at him that made contact she noticed some paper in the back. It read:

Paper Note

The white sheet
Is calling me
Tempting me to write
Sitting, Planning,
Luring me
To open my mind to your sight
Does it want me to write?
About why
I always sat alone?
How I was left out
Happy when no one was home
About how I was criticized
Just a young child
When I got picked on
Fought them; whipped them
But never I cried
Or was it why
I grew up too fast
My childhood in a blur
How long did that last?
Seen too much
Obscene too much
Been there, done that
But it's still not enough
I've been walking too long
And I've been walking much farther
I've fallen down so much

That I've got to work harder
Do you rather want
Me to write
About what I see?
A million faces in the crowd
See them...hear them taping their feet
It's all chaos
And anarchy is how it's spelt
Being the underdog in a million
Imagine how that must have felt
I will write about the time
I fell in love and when I fell alone
How high I rose...how high I flew
Stronger than the stars I shone
It was an act of mutilation
True pain I felt
Why walk among million I thought
Fly above them, but now I knelt
I lost in love, I lost in life
I lost in what I set
I fell alone, unsure ...in doubt
Boldly smiling...silently I slept
What do you want me to write oh paper?
With my back against the wall
Should I laugh or cry oh paper
....should I write at all

It stopped her in her tracks; she folded the paper and took her clothes to change in the next room. Rahul entered covering her with a blanket, "you'll catch a cold" he said hugging her.

There were no lights on, just the heat. Megha liked it that way and as Rahul's warm body heated her she felt relaxed and happy. He took her next to the window wrapping her up in the blanket and keeping her in his arms. They saw the clouds float lazily past by the window, the valley now completely dark had a few lights on; the cloudy mist put all activity to rest.

It was rare for the mist to come out in the evening hours, but as Megha sat there looking at it flowing through the valley she reflected on the past year. It had been nothing short of an adventure, full of countless clashes of opinion, ideologies, and so many crazy incidents. It was time well spent, it was life well lived.

Rahul was different: different bad and different good. She had started to find the man in the pages, slowly close to the amour he had put up, but she knew he was there. There was as much darkness as there was life in the man, sometimes she was all his and sometimes she could feel the difference.

He had told her about this and warned her that she may not like what she found once she came too close. It was never a decision for Megha to think about, she knew what she wanted.

She caressed his arm, 'this is a writer's arm,' inked on it. It contrasted against his skin.

"Are you happy?" she asked him.

"Why would you doubt it, happy as a clam" his arms tightened around her.

She could tell the difference, today he was hers. There was always restlessness inside him, as if a fire burnt inside him. The detachment, it killed her sometimes but it was adorable how he would try and compensate for all those times, in his own little ways and gestures. Some girls could only hope for things like that. He was flawed, severely, but in a way not every man is.

"I saw the poem you hid in the closet."

"I write stuff, and that was from a long time ago. Just found it.

There was honesty in what he said, Megha made herself more comfortable in his arms. The room was full of books and canvas, oil paints spread over the room, this was his getaway place, there was something soothing about the place.

Not very long ago Rahul had finished the painting he had been working on for some days, he hardly slept while painting, he would paint and smoke and paint. But tonight he slept like a child in deep sleep. It was a particularly cold night and the electricity had just come and the house had just started to heat again. She remembered what he had said "what use is the rain if you are always dry, what good is the cold if you are always warm?" she had suspected that Bob Marley had said that but it was true no matter who said it.

Her eyes burning for sleep but her mind would not stop working. She looked at the painting he had finished. It greatly amused her that every piece he wrote, every painting he completed it would always be something she would not be expecting, it always took her time to understand and even then there would be something more to it. 'Once in a party' was scribbled in the bottom corner. It was a painting of a glass reflecting hundreds of colors perched at the edge of a wall and darkness behind it. It made her think she didn't understand him at all; there were only so many things you could understand! The man was crazy, with too many stories to tell and very few ears to listen. She always felt he was wasting away doing whatever he was with his life. She knew he felt the same way but it was life, and it was reality, the only thing that is omnipotent and omnipresent: Reality. He had made his decisions and now was living through them.

Her thoughts went to the article she had done recently, the death of handmade pottery in the country. She had gone to a village famous for pottery and found it really, dying. There were signs of celebrations but they seemed faded and out of place now.

The articles that they had made were to come out perfect, else they were worthless. If there was too much water, too much heat, too much mixing it would be useless. It had become almost impossible to sell the articles now, no one bothered about such fragile articles.

But everything is fragile, the lamp, dreams, ideas, men, talent. Reality was the only thing that lived on. She looked at Rahul sleeping in a funny way; it was surprising how well he had turned considering he came out burnt, charred and wobbly.

Morning came and Rahul woke up early. He searched for Megha; she was not in the bed. He saw her sleeping on the patio bundled in a pile of blankets. He unwrapped her face from the layers of blankets.

"What" the angry face asked him.

"It is morning."

"So?"

"So get up, you have to do your article remember?"

The angry face looked at him.

"Get me some coffee, and then we will talk."

It would be a cold day again Rahul thought as he heated the milk. He had a sleepless night, no dreams, and no restlessness. He was happy. He felt different, normal, and simple. The place always made him feel that way and Megha had been such a wonderful addition to it. He wanted to change, from the schizoid product that was left after the fight between idealism and reality. He deserved a chance to be happy. He brought coffee to the bundle of blankets on the patio and a pair of eyes peeked through them.

"How did you end up here anyway?"

"Was looking out the window, guess I fell asleep. You finished the painting."

"Yeah, something from long ago."

They were soon traveling in his jeep through the hilly terrain to the animal shelter. She interviewed the owner, asked him about the sponsors, how those animals were brought there, what medical assistance they get, if there were any endangered species, taking notes in her notebook. She was brain storming, how to frame the article, what would be its theme, who should it be reaching out to.

She saw Rahul playing with the animals; a parrot was trying to take his cap as dogs were gunning for his attention. It was such a funny sight as he saw her looking he gave her thumbs up and restored to trying to save his cap.

It was a couple of hours after which Megha had enough material to work on her article, it was the clash of abandonment and care that had attracted her to this story, how one part of the world can leave these animals to the open world when they became an inconvenience or a hindrance to them, maybe they were someone's pets maybe they were strays…they were taken care of now. They were taken care of now by also people, the irony of it. They were driving back to the apartment through narrow roads in the middle of the forest. It was a beautiful day and the valley below where they drove into, a sleepy place with simple folks. The roads from the hills spilling into the valley, Rahul driving the jeep seemed pre occupied, he hadn't said a word since they left shelter, "those animals looked as if they wanted to keep you" Megha said to him coyly, Rahul smiled but said nothing. "That parrot seemed fond of you" she said "it just wouldn't get off of your shoulder," Rahul just smiled and laughed but said nothing and they kept driving. It troubled Megha; his silence was nothing alarming but unsettling for her. It could just be that he was tired or maybe thinking about something, Megha remembered the poem that was sitting on the bed the night before, he had said he had written it before; Rahul hadn't written any poems in the past year Megha had been with him. A small sonnet to cheer her up or a rhyme to get himself out of trouble but nothing he would call a poem or anything he would write in the small black book he had, the one captioned 'Fairy Tales', Megha's thoughts brought her back to the book every time Rahul sat quietly or looked away pensively. She felt the urgency to do something to make him feel better; she just wasn't sure what was better for him. She had relied on the small book of poems as a friend, finding Rahul was nothing less than impossible but there he sat. She knew Rahul now, bits and pieces of him. The poem had been particularly grim, like a frustrated cry of a prisoner in a cell. 'Cellar door' she had read somewhere were the two words put together that displayed a huge human emotion; the door out of confinement into the outside world. The cry of the prisoner is either of why he is in there or why he wants to get out. Solitude often breaks the man. Sometimes it makes one stronger.

"Rahul are you ok?" Megha finally said, Rahul looked at her eyebrows raised. "Yeah, I'm good" returning back to the road, one thing Megha had noticed about him was that he can be a liar, a good one but the kind who doesn't lie to you to hurt you, but lies to protect himself, in his own way. Megha wasn't convinced, "what are you thinking about?" She asked. His eyes twitched but he didn't say anything. "Tell me" Megha said looking at him, Rahul turning the jeep through the tiny degrading road still made no reply. "Is it about the poem?" she wasn't giving up easily, not this time. Rahul looked at her with a pained expression, and then looked away. "Stop the car" Megha said looking straight at him; he parked the jeep near a small clearing off the road only a few minutes away from the valley now. Her hand was on his shoulder as the jeep ceased making noise; the day was already giving way for the night as the sky was painted with a dark blue. "Why did you write that poem Rahul, are you unhappy? I don't understand," Megha said. Rahul looked at her with the same pained expression, as if he was apologizing in a way for whatever he felt or whatever he was going to say. "I am happy" Rahul said slowly, "that's the problem", he waited for a moment for it to sink in, Megha's expression did not betray her confusion, Rahul continued slowly "I was not made in a way; that I stay happy." He paused; eyes fixed somewhere a foot away from Megha's face. "The fire Megha" said Rahul "It's not that simple" he said. "It's getting dark", he said bringing the jeep back to life, and Megha sat there trying to understand what had just happened. As they drove back home no one spoke. They entered the apartment, there was no electricity and the room was as dark as they had left it. Megha sat at the patio near the window. With Rahul in the other room washing him up, Megha picked up the poem which she had seen, she did not want to be upset, and she wasn't going to be irrational about this. She knew Rahul, she knew him even before she had met him and she had found him not very different. Megha lights a cigarette and reads the poem again. She exhaled smoke as she read it. "Why does he have to be so cryptic all the time, the fire? What does that mean?"Megha mutters to herself as she finds herself in the same position she had been a year ago, trying to decipher the meaning of line and words. The mobile phone besides her buzzed 'boss calling' flashed on the screen." Megha is that article ready?" the voice belonged to a certain Mr. Jas, her team leader. The editor was obviously making more important decisions and had assigned Mr. Jas to deal with the smaller ones. "I have the material, by when do you want me to send it in?"," I want it by tonight, I have two more articles in hand but this article fits in with our recent reports, people keep writing in about the dog story we ran last week, people love animal shit. Send it by 10 no latter; mail it to me so I can give it a read through before I send it forward". Megha checked her watch, it was only 7, "sure Jas, I will mail it right away". Megha hung up taking another drag on her now dying cigarette. Keeping the paper in her hand aside she picked up her laptop opening her note book.

Rahul entered the room watching Megha open up her laptop, he could smell smoke in the room, he felt the familiar burning feeling inside him; probing him, pushing him into darkness, and he won't let that happen. Not today.

"Hey, workaholic how come you getting started on that report already, isn't it due, well in a million years; said Rahul sitting on the chair opposite the patio. "This is for the paper;

they decided to run this tomorrow, need to send it in before 10" said Megha not looking up from the screen. Rahul was glad she was doing something to keep her busy; he had his demons gnawing on him. "Anything I can do to help?" he asked. "Get us some dinner will you?" Megha said deep inside her notes, flipping pages and noting it on the laptop not looking up. "Sure" he stood up. Then she looked up and catching his eyes she smiled pausing for a little while "come back fast" she said, as if she was going to say something else. Rahul smiled at her, his demons backing away from him for the moment. Walking away from the room he felt as if everything had frozen suddenly; everything, breath, time, reality.

He took his jacket and walked out of the house. It hit him slowly as he walked in the now dark empty street. The chill traced through his body, he was familiar with the feeling, the clarity, and the blood rushing through him; something prodding him, probing him to work for the cause; the people passing by him in the dark street; 'walkers'. They walked past him and the great tree canvassing the dark sky sent another shiver down his spine. This is how he saw it, the understanding about the world, the need for free thought, the need to defy the tree, his wings, all these thoughts came rushing back to him, rushing though they had never gone; but they were back again.

His mind jumping a hundred places and to a hundred ideas at the same time, all with the same intention, to free himself from the land of these walkers, to wake everyone up to the reality of the great tree, to use all mediums at his disposal to convey the message, the flight waited him, his wings aching to reveal themselves, aching to fly.

He could not do it.

He was no longer sure; the fire had burnt him too many times. Why should he, why HIM? It was not fair, he had his flight, and the taste of it sometimes still lingered on his tongue. But it was a long time ago. This was his life now. Now was his life, not in the past. In the past one year many things had changed. He was happy. He had never been happy, never belonged anywhere. He was happy now, he belonged somewhere now; with Megha on his side he had found the world much more of an acceptable place to live in. He had finally accepted the roots he had grown on the ground that they kept him where maybe he was meant to be. The tree was too great to oppose, it had been impossible from the start, he had just started realizing it now. He was tired of the flame licking his insides, not letting him live his time through, he had fallen many years ago and life was finally catching up with him now. He wanted to be normal, as normal as the shopkeeper who gave him his food in a parcel package, as normal as the couple he brushed by walking out of the store. His eyes were aching; the clarity always left his body weakened. The poem he had found the other day was from a long time ago. It cried desperation as the clarity ran though him; he was just a child then trying his best to make his way past the confines that bound him. He did not want to be unhappy anymore. He wanted to have a chance at having a normal life without having its reality flashed at him, without the greater questions hounding him, without the need to find the answers probing him, without the haunting restlessness not letting him sleep at night. He had fought the battle, it was over. It was life over fantasy now, life is no fairy tale. Maybe this is how it is supposed to be. Maybe there are no answers in life. Maybe….he was the one who was different in a land of normal people. Maybe…..

Parting Ways

As he walked inside opening the door there was light coming from the room, there finally was electricity in the place. Rahul placed the parcel on the table and moved inside the room; there were lit candles scattered all over the room, over the small rickety table, over the floor, around the bed; on which sat Megha. She sat in her night gown, her long legs folded together stuck out; the gown was all that she was wearing. Rahul moved closer to the bed with his eyes meeting Megha's, his eyes fixed into hers. "I got dinner..." said Rahul as he moved closer to the bed. Megha looked at him with a slight mischievous smile dancing on her lips, a beckoning smile. Rahul makes his way to the bed, their eyes meet; and then their lips meet. It was a soft warm kiss. As he pulls her closer she kisses him harder. Their breath races as the urgency becomes clear and their senses take over.

"What about your report?" asked Rahul with Megha cradled in his arms just as he had recovered his breath. It was warm between both of them, bundled up in sheets completely oblivious of the cold night outside.

"Done, sent and he loved it" mumbled Megha. She felt warm in his arms as her head rested on his shoulder; she was clutching him and drifting to sleep. He looked at her; she looked so beautiful in the moonlight which spilt through the window. He gently ran his hands through her hair, slowly caressing her. The moment right there was perfect; he gently kissed her forehead and tightened his arms around her. She looked up and smiled at him; she reached up and kissed him.

They just looked at each other for some time, neither one of them wanting to ruin the moment. She finally asked smiling at Rahul "I thought you brought some food."

Rahul stifling a yawn nodded smiling, "yep, it would be cold by now."

"Weren't expecting this were you" asked Megha coyly.

"Part of me is always expecting this" replied Rahul grinning at her.

Megha hit Rahul, not as lightly as one would expect a girl to and she got up wrapping the sheet around her. She sat looking outside the window; it had troubled her that Rahul was suffering with whatever that takes him away from her and only a disconnected shell of a person is left behind. He did not need to do it alone now. She snuggled up with Rahul as they both sat staring out of the window, the candles burning their life away into a dim glow in the room. Rahul lit a cigarette and he slowly took a drag as he caressed Megha with the other hand, she was with him, he was happy, there were no demons asking more of him. He was content being just a man, content being just alive; content with being a small part of an insignificant world. As the smoke blew up in a cloud away from him he felt the day take its toll on him, the clarity had left his body weak. He looked at the open sky hoping that someone would do what he could not. He stubbed the cigarette and caressed Megha till she fell asleep. Rahul looked around in the now dark room as the candles had sang their last goodbye and had slept, to the dark room he smiled a small painful smile and closed his weary eyes.

Morning came with a blinding sunlight, which was very uncommon in the area. Megha had woke him up with coffee. They both were starved and so got down to the nearest café, where they had spent many evenings and early mornings planning the day, the places to visit and taking a break from the day in the end. It was time to leave the small apartment and return back to normal day life. Megha had been assigned study and report assignments in the hilly area by her professor Mr. Trivedi, he was an unconventional teacher and a strange person but he had been one of the greatest reporters in his time and a very influential person once. Though Megha had finished her degree Mr. Trivedi had separated her and assigned her to the case, Megha did not ask many questions because somehow the person inspired her to push herself and work. For her he represented every quality why she wanted to become a journalist. She had regularly been reporting to him about the different topics she had chosen to research on. He had guided her through the entire process pushing her to develop and explore different angles of the same topic, to bring out not just the news but also the essence of the story in the same lines using the same words, he had greatly influenced her writing and considered herself lucky to have found such an oddity of a teacher and such a genius of a person. Mr. Trivedi was the one who had brought her to the job of training journalist, it provided her with the freedom of pursuing the story she wanted and no pressure of reporting only the story the media was blazing with. "There will always be enough moths to keep hitting the glowing lamp in the night, only the brave firefly tries to illuminate the darkness with her own light" she remembered him saying to her. Rahul had agreed to take her to his place in the mountains rather he had suggested it. Megha had said yes immediately, she trusted Rahul completely and she was a big girl now, she knew how to take care of herself. Though having an athletically built companion around didn't hurt.

The past weeks they had spent hunting down leads on stories Megha and Mr Trivedi had decided upon. There was so much hidden in the lives of the simple people that it made one wonder how shallow lives people were living in cities where gadgets and money mattered more than humans.

There they sat, finally the assignment period was over and even Rahul had to return to his work. He was sipping his second coffee and nibbling his scrambled eggs as Megha arranged her papers. She would return to her apartment in the city she had taken with Candy and Anagha. Her room mates were the best people to be flat mates with she had decided. Her own little life waited for her back home. She would visit her parents the next weekend; it had been ages since she had visited home. Both her parents were more than happy that she had finished her degree and already was working, she had so often heard the anxiousness in their voice spiked with pride, and they were so adorable she missed them already. She looked across at Rahul devouring his food now; she wondered where he would return to, where did his parents live? What kind of people were they? What kind of friends did he have? How was he around them? He had always been just him, and for her it had always been more than enough, she worried for him though. He seemed different when he came back last night, more humane almost. She did not feel him holding back as if he was afraid to reach out for her, she had felt so loved. It was good but it wasn't like Rahul, she wasn't sure if it were a good thing or a bad thing...

"I am going to miss this place" Megha said looking across to Rahul.

"You can always come back whenever you want" Rahul replied sipping his coffee.

"Let's see when that happens" she said "not that you would get it Tin Man" she added coyly.

"Not that person anymore" he said smiling at her.

Megha could not understand what he meant by that. She stared at him. "Where are you going to return to?"She asked him.

"Work"

"After that"

"Work"

"No going home?"

"I will, it's been long."

"When will I see you?"

"Sooner than you expect."

Megha laughed, she had expected him to get all awkward at that question, and she was not expecting that answer.

"Really? Honest word?" She asked.

Rahul nodded, they soon took all their belongings and were on their way to civilization. They took different trains from the station, Megha had tears in her eyes as she hugged him but she smiled at him as they said their farewells, she left him with a wet kiss on his cheek. He stood on the station for a little while and then went to his train.

Cellar Door

Towards the horizon
With shield and sword
To fight we march as one
In a legion of warriors
All lovers of death
I stand ahead the chosen one

I hear the footsteps
Of an angry beast approaching
To even the greatest it is a formidable sound
As they come to sight
Burning the ground, ready to fight
Scattering dusty smoke all around

Even as fear pricks me
I roar: men today we fight!
We shall not fall
And they will bleed
Our swords will blind the sun!
Live for glory and die for glory
For a glorious death is next to none!!
We charge on to battle
With our eyes set on blood
As the sword clashes against metal
You can hear death laughing from above

I bleed and cut
Taunting them to give up
I go in deeper; foolishly
And find myself surrounded

I swing my sword
And charge at them
With a roar I rip open their hearts
Leaving them dead, astounded

Just then in the heat and dust
An arrow cuts through my skin
And a club finds my head
I lose sight and the air gets thin
I wake up to find
My arms wrapped in chains
Me a man of honour
There is no bigger shame!

I shall not bend
And I shall not break
My life they can have
My glory they will not take

I stare at it
I deserve death in battle and more!
I stare at it,
My greatest rival of all
I stare at the cellar door

Months became years
And I know our siege must have failed
For I rot in this cellar

With no light to fall on my face
I beg for the rain to find me
Make their way, on my face
Once again, I beg the winds to take
All their sweetness
And life that they bring
And fill my tiny cellar
To remind me of the man I had once been

Years gone by now just an old man
A fool, a vain warrior now wasted
By his pride, just a puppet
A tool, a pawn on the field
The warrior turns philosopher
Yet this door does not budge
The cellar door stares at him in silence
As animated as it ever was

He dies as an old man
Oh so horribly alone
Remembering in his last breath
The battles he had won
They came to claim his body
And one spoke to another
He was a great warrior I hear
Killed as many as any ever could
Who knew the one to slay him?
Would be this rod of metal
And a five inches door of wood.

Elemental Family

Rahul returned to his work, he was trying to be a different person now and there would always be more than enough people to work with, he closed his laptop and took his coat; it was time.

He faced the scenery ahead of him. The grass was still green and the stones were still holding their ground sturdy and strong. The wearing of the years seemed almost graceful on the scene. Below in the valley stood a castle, tall and welcoming. He slowly started walking into the valley and made his way to the castle.

Familiar scenes flashed pass by him. He moved through them not disturbing the surroundings, he made his way unnoticed. Not much had changed only spread out more. Walkers everywhere, Just as he had remembered it. The market place, the crossings the small shops were as sleepy as he had left them. He finally stood at the entrance of the castle, the castle of King Stone and Lady River.

King Stone, the great. Just his presence would turn any walker to shame. He was the embodiment of virtue and strength. The boy tightened his fist as he prepared to face him. Lady River as the name suggested was as harsh and as calm as the mighty river, the boy did not know anyone till now who could deter her path.

The boy's adventures, his solace, his darkness seemed small and he could not feel his demons gnawing at him. The aura of the place seemed to push away the darkness, something he was afraid of. He did not know if he would be pushed away by the aura. The dark thoughts in him seemed no longer to be there, he felt small.

The gate opened and the boy was led through the path to meet him. King Stone looked at the boy and gasped. King Stone walked up to the boy looming over him, his face lined and his features chiselled; strong defiant of years he stood there and then embraced him

"Welcome home, son."

He embraced King Stone, his father and smiled at him; the aura of strength around him made the boy feel reassured. Lady River flooded the room and swept him away, as she always did. She splashed him with embraces and love; she caressed him, as gentle waves do to a person who had washed up in the sea. There was silence then as she tumbled away to bring him water. That was Lady River, his mother.

They sat down in his home, the small castle in the middle of nowhere. It was quiet and clean and after a long time the boy with the broken wings could sigh and just be. He looked around as his parents sat beside him, Lady River asking, talking to him, asking him, scolding him all with twinkling eyes and a smile that said she still couldn't believe he was home. King Stone sat on his throne and just observed him, he had a smile on his face that would be of nothing less than of pride, his son had come home after all.

In all the years he had seen the boy growing up. He remembered the time the boy was born and stared at him with his big eyes, he laughed every time he thought about that day, something had changed ever since. Watching the boy grow up was to grow up; in the years a man has had to raise a son. Life is something to unravel something to understand, there is a beginning and an end to everything including the simple human body and this journey to another realm, a sanctum for absolution from the riddles of birth and death, from sins of us and our forefathers. The journey is a lonely one and one has to rid himself of temptation, desire, fear, greed, envy, and pride and bear our share of burden. I am King Stone, and I will be there for this child when he calls upon me.

Their eyes met and spoke a thousand words.

The boy had one hinge between his ideals and the real world, King Stone. He stood there as a contradiction to all his accusations and an icon for all he stood for. He was the knowledge that is present in the edges of the universe; he has the answer to the questions. No he isn't perfect, he is just a man, he has his limits, but if there ever were a man to respect, a man to be a king as strong, as dependable, as noticeable a presence it would be him, King Stone. Again they stood at logger heads, the boy who wanted to fly and the king who stood as steadfast as stone.

Lady River smiled and caressed his hair. The boy looked at her and nothing could stop him from embracing her, his friend, consultant, and mother. He was more like his mother than he realized. It was she who wrote, she who always had a flare for literature, she who was the rebel. She was as beautiful as he always remembered her to be yet more graceful and elegant. How she did it was a secret she never told him. She always did have an air of mystique about her, with her little tricks and her small surprises and a witty answer for every question and a quick repartee for every statement. She was the standard he titrated perfection against.

Just as he had sat down and taken a breath he felt something was missing from the castle and sure enough felt the prickling drops of water fall on him despite the walls and the roof, the rain got harder and harder as there were no roofs that could keep this rain away; each drop stronger and faster than the one before it. All of them alone and cold but strong as they fell together; he saw his sister the Rain as she entered the room, her presence preceding her arrival. She smacked him square on his head as they began their session of pulling legs and name calling.

Yes, now he was finally home.

As the train rocked away slowly from the platform Megha dissolved into her own train of thoughts, her thoughts took her to Rahul as they almost always did nowadays. "Not the same man anymore" she remembered him saying and the change in his persona she had noticed, Megha wondered what he had met. Knowing him for more than two years it was as if she had known him her entire life, reading those poems had changed her life in so many ways. She was able to break from the strands which would have tied her down to such a smaller view of life; "enslaved by the great tree" she could almost hear him say. Fate had not been as kind on him, he never had anyone to guide him into breaking free from the picture frame of the obvious he had paved his own way by his hardships, his failures, his losses, his wins, by daring to think different and choosing to act on his beliefs. There were so many dimensions to the things we blindly walk past by, and the subtlety and beauty in them which the normal eye would never see. It was difficult to say what Rahul's demons were, he had told her very plainly that he had absence of emotions or rather a scarcity of them, that he understood the far spanning possibilities that were present and could do little about them, his burning need to wake up every dormant happy mind and show them the spectrum of choices waiting for them but more than anything Megha knew that Rahul wanted to know the answers to all the bigger question of life and not in a compromising or ambiguous manner. He would never give up on trying to understand and challenge the limitations that have been handed down to us, he would never stop looking at the reason for things the way they are and how can they be improved or changed. He and Megha had spoken into many nights right through to the crack of dawn and those talks were nothing apart from a calibration to the truth of things from her own picture of it, he had told her simply as if it were something he had known his entire life " the horizontal life is endless, there will always be greed, ambition to shepherd you into the next new thing and this life is so intricately spread that it can keep you engrossed, captured by its complexity; you could have spent your entire life in any manner you wanted without even thinking twice. But that is the worst crime one can do to himself, there is a life in the vertical. Yes, a life in which your decisions are not made on the basis of the carrot that is hanging in front of you but to answer the bigger questions in life like why, where, how? Can it really be true that billions of people live without them wondering why we are here? Is it possible that the only reason for our existence is to obtain a comfortable life? How can it be correct, that we sit in oblivion and fight for dominance? What is worse than all of this is that so many people cannot or do not want to ask themselves these questions. "Think Megha, make your peace with it but I am afraid I never will be able to....it is kind of too late for that." He smiled as he finished, he then got off track and continued on making a string of poor jokes and retelling tales of his past which were sometimes hard to believe. Megha sometimes stopped listening to what he was saying and kept looking at him ramble on, he was so graphic and fluid in his talk, he seemed so happy for some reason when he spoke to her. There was something really soothing about that, all tough and brooding sometimes and happy as a kid sometimes she couldn't help but think there was something missing in him that would bridge these different poles of behaviors.

What was Rahul's problem? It was that he had all the ideas on the earth but nowhere to go with them, a deep sense of liberation and value of life but trapped in a place and time where no one wanted to be alive, he wanted to fly as he keeps saying but it isn't all imagination.

It was something Megha could understand now after reading all those poems and listening to him and spending time with him she understood that it wasn't just a moan of frustration which she had heard from many people , but it was almost as if he was bidding for his time , waiting for something. She didn't understand him still, there was still something that he was withholding from her it could be a lot more that he wasn't letting on to her and she would not know. It was a different experience being with that person and she knew Rahul thought the same way about her. He kept testing her in little ways in the start and through the middle till the time she told him that he had nothing to worry about and it was okay, regardless of whatever was wrong. He slept like a baby that night as she remembered it.

The train stopped and she got off squinting her eyes as the now awake sun poured down sunshine on everyone. She saw her mother standing looking for her. Megha smiled and started walking towards her.

After being at home it almost seemed that she had fallen off a mountain, every muscle in her body ached as she slept through most of the day. Only in evening of the next day it would seem that she could peep out of her room again.

She hadn't told anyone that she was returning home from her trip and she hadn't told anyone she had gone with Rahul. She sipped her evening coffee in her dimly lit room in the evening and logged into her computer. Her friends said hello (more like heeeeeeeeeeeeyyyyy!!!!!!!!!!!), some said hello in their own style but all of them wanted to meet her, above all Mr. Trivedi. She had mailed him his article and he had said he wanted to meet her to give the feedback, she was eager to take his insight into her work.

Mr. Trivedi sat in his cabin alone in the university, he was old and a little strange but a brilliant man who had degrees in psychology, journalism and was very affluent in his times. They sat and discussed the article, he looked at her and said that the work was different from her usual style and was better than the level of the university paper, he would see that it reaches the best platform was what he promised her. Megha hesitated for a second and Mr. Trivedi caught on to that "tell me" he said closing his books and keeping aside the article. Megha told him in concise about Rahul and his work and that how she thought it was something which could amount to something to something great. Mr. Trivedi asked her to send a sample of his work and that he could judge it himself. Megha kept the small leather bound ugly book on his table, he read the prologue and the first few pages, his brows almost colliding with each other he continued to read through the book as Megha went and got herself some lunch when she returned she saw him in complete submersion of the poems and the book, "Mr. Trivedi? I got you some lunch" after a few moments he looked at her with complete honesty in his eyes "this scares me."

"What?"

"These words, the man behind the words is not a man at all, he craves to be human and feels the same thing we all do but he can only try...he has nothing to lose and he knows that. People like this end up either as martyrs or murderers; when they can't feel anything at all it reaches a point where a more violent and aggressive behavior pattern can emerge dominating whatever personality the person had evolved into. His is a good liar probably a very intelligent man. Does this person live alone? Is he withdrawn, sad? Why do you think that is?"

Megha was stunned and didn't know what to say, he had never laid a hand on her or made her feel as if she was under threat, he was always almost...too good to be true. He wasn't a monster waiting to burst out in the world neither was he going to die in vain, he was smarter than that but she couldn't help but think there was a reality she was too naïve to understand. The wings, the tree, the flight all of it now seemed as a mechanism to compensate for him being different, for him trying to be human or whatever he thought human was. The 'Fairy Tales' he wrote were of his own mind battling to be different and at the same time; being normal. He was waiting for something; she had always thought... maybe he was waiting for this conflict to stop..... "I am happy...that's the problem", "the fire Megha...it's not that simple". Cold chills began running through Megha's body as it all came crashing down upon her, all those things he said all the times he behaved so happily with helpless animals and so indifferent and hostile to common people, how there were scars he had inflicted upon himself as punishment. Maybe she had finally begun to understand Rahul's problem.

Megha would not let this transformation happen to Rahul, there were two poles in his personality; yes the innocent little boy and the cold indifferent adult. "Martyr or murderer" the words rang in her head. Urgency had struck Megha and she did not know what to do..." he needs help" then she said to Mr. Trivedi sitting in front of her. "He is smart enough to know the problem and by now he had made up his mind as well....treatment and reforms would only trigger his aggressive behavior further."

"His poems, his books, his painting....I want to get them printed...for him to see that his words can bring a change... that's what he wants..."

"Then why hasn't he gotten them printed already dear?"

It had never occurred to her...he had always stirred away from the topic and she had always been so captivated in trying to decipher what it was...she had been so naïve.....

"His thoughts have transcended into a different sphere where humanity is broken down to its naked core, I'm very sure he often wonders if it's even trying to 'save' humanity, or to wake them up or try and do anything about them at all," Mr. Trivedi finished looking intently at the book in front of him.

"And that was when he wrote the book...judging by its shape I say it's rather old, since then I cannot say what kind of person he has chosen to become but you can and will notice that there will be flaws in whatever he is projecting himself to be...there will be inconsistencies in his behavior almost as if something was missing..." what he said struck too close to home.

Megha left him sitting in his cabin as she took the book away from him, she had not yet decided if he had gotten carried away or had she been ignorant all this time. More importantly if Rahul would ever commit a murder or die for a vain cause, there was a very less chance of both of them happening but she had broken through into the darker side of Rahul today finally and it scared her; what she had found. She understood it now the small black book was more than a spark thrown into chaos it was a cry for help, or companionship but there was a grey shade behind all his talks of liberation and freedom because all he wanted was to not be alone. He had not finished his flight because there were still things which kept him to the ground...under the protection of the great tree...maybe he was afraid to fly away.....

Megha did not know what to do...she wanted to be with him as a friend a lover but that would only trap him into the state of conflict he was in...he would try with all his sincerity to love her as she loved him...but there would always be a wall he would not be able to cross...he would compensate with his little ways but she did not want to put him in a state of constant struggle to be with her how she needed him to be, she could not, it wouldn't be fair...but she needed him as much as he needed her. She was better with him and he with her...it was different. She loved him with all his little quirks, she loved his thoughts, and how he had painted for her, written for her... made her so much better than she would have been without him...she was alone and sad but he had brought so much into her life....

It was days before she had made up her mind...but it was what she had decided...it was for the best.

Pages from Rahul's Diary

Compartmentalize.

The ability to store information in a box, label it and keep in memory. This is a very much desired attribute for certain memory techniques; to relate certain objects in order to learn their sequence etc. The brain becomes a storage unit for different bits of info, which come forward when the need for the similar situation arrives, that much part of memory is activated and 'viola.'

However the technique when extended to real life situations leads to a condition of being able to convince oneself about the reality of the events. Memories can be stored and kept away to continue doing what one is set to; making you impervious to weaknesses and setbacks not permanently however. This can often be referred to as running away from problems but this largely relies on the will power of the individual. By using this, one gets time to take care of issues and problems but if one can be caught in a delusion where one may feel in charge but in all true respects is- fucked.

This method is widely diverse in every individual in terms of how they choose to implement it. Serial killers are attributed the tendency to behave normal in front of others in order to avoid getting caught or arousing suspicion. The trick here is to convince yourself that you are innocent and develop a story to fool your own subconscious in order to fully act on that story and avoid the truth in the source of its storage in the mind.

This process of perception of daily activities can cause a sense of alienation and numbness to situations which otherwise would be troubling or emotional. This feeling of numbness develops, which eventually will even begin to form another source of perception of the incident.

How can a man get caught while telling a lie if he himself cannot tell the difference? The most important thing is to remember that it is a skill that stays with you like a bad addiction and would take serious efforts to remove from your system. Imagine if you can harm a person and never remember that you did it, wouldn't it just be the perfect crime in your eyes. One can pursue anything with extreme ruthlessness and never remember things he doesn't want to. Some people kill out of need, some out of desperation but most kill for the thrill of it, to throw away the chains of emasculation and let the thrill flow through them, now if these people kill and never remember doing it then they would have had the thrill but no stains on their conscience and they will kill again and again because there is no regret or remorse to counter it. Some learn or develop this skill and some are born with it. It is as much as a curse as it is a gift, sometimes I too think if I can kill a person and not feel anything. I think I can, but there is neither any need nor a situation where I need to go chasing a thrill. Along with the ability to compartmentalize, the quality of detachment acts as a deadly combination, no, literally. Though I feel no such need to kill but sadly I know it's a feature in me that I can at best ignore and not think about.

Spiritual Experience

Megha said good bye to her parents as she was returning to her apartment with her friends. Her work was about to start soon and there were things to settle and finish before that. In her apartment both Anagha and Candy were waiting for her, they wanted to know about what she had been up to. Everything seemed to just pass in motions and she could pay little attention to the things as they went by, the revelations about Rahul and herself had taken a toll on Megha…she brooded on almost everything…every moment she could remember having spent with him and knew that there was some truth to what Mr. Trivedi had said…but she also knew that Rahul would never turn into the monster Mr. Trivedi had predicted him to be…he had changed… he had told Megha he wasn't the same person anymore when she had called him 'Tin Man'…was he so capable of shifting into another personality? Was that acceptable? What would happen in the future? There were so many thoughts and questions that plagued her mind and her conscience that she became withdrawn from her surroundings.

Rahul showed up one fine morning at Megha's apartment. Megha was shocked to see him but she had missed him so much she was very happy. She hugged him tightly and brought him in to introduce to Anagha and Candy. They had breakfast which Rahul cooked for everyone and then he took her out for a movie...it was evening when they returned to her apartment. " You can crash at the couch if you want" Megha said coyly and suggestively to him as they came near the door...she had almost forgotten about the last few days and the decision she had made...it struck her then as Rahul smiled and said it was no problem. The feeling of being aloof reminded her of everything Mr. Trivedi had said... .."Rahul...I want to talk...let's go to the roof."

Megha was in tears by the time it was over and Rahul had given no expression at all....

"It's for your good Rahul..."

"You don't worry about that anymore, he said in a cold and stable voice.

"Whatever you have said is true and I don't blame you... It was my foolishness for getting too attached to you, I did not want this for you...You are a beautiful girl and probably deserve and will get better."

He walked away from the cold roof where it had begun raining...Megha stayed on the roof...crying. Rahul rang her apartment bell and told Anagha that Megha was crying on the roof. She immediately rushed up. Rahul collected his belongings and left.

Rahul felt calm and in his element, he knew whatever she had said was true, it has crossed his mind several times as well and it was better that he left her alone...as he drove his bike back into the night he felt something strange...pain. It pained him; almost as if he were sad.

There was nothing to feel sad about; this had to happen one day or the other. It was a cold night but yet young and the wicked deserve no rest.

There was no tree in Rahul's life nor were there wings or flight...there were lakes of brown liquid and spirits of red and black ...flowing through the ground and he had found his own dark corner in it...there was always a misty smoke all around the scene and he could not see . The spirits coaxed and loved him as the sirens do, they ran through him and made his senses placid and under a trance, the powerful spirits neat and immaculate ran down him sometimes as cold as ice other times burning him inside out. The cold dark lake saw through him night after night but the small pain in him would not go away...they swayed him and rowed him into the lake of abyss and oblivion where finally maybe he would be at peace, with no betrayal and loneliness to pull him apart and no questions keeping him up at night. He was stronger than the spirits but he wanted them to sedate him and intoxicate him with all their glamour their glass bodies offered for it was time to see this through to the end. His breathing was ragged and forced, he knew he would now reach a point where there was no returning from and it was okay, he was ready and looking forward to it. There was nothing to lose and nothing to mourn the spirits told him, there was only bliss and slumber waiting.

He had gone too deep into the trance as the spirits of insidious intentions rowed him into the lake of oblivion, to its dead center. He slipped into its spirited depths never to remember the sky. It was then when he closed his eyes and let go of his final breaths that he heard something.

It was Rain...he came to the surface and saw the Rain spreading the brown liquid of the lake, gushing the spirits away, weakening their hold on him. The lake fought back as it had claimed him now...simple rain could not match something so powerful and ancient. forcefully pure water from the River gushed into the lake...punishing the brown ancient away from its strong hold, Lady River would have no one damn him just yet...the spirits yet hissed and fought back from its deep evil core to not leave what was hers, now the River smacked them away and they dissolved in the River's sheer volume and resolve. The deep evil of the lake pushed forward and denied the Rain and the River of the boy pulling him under deeper and deeper into its viscous folds, towards its unfathomable depths. There was a long strong roar which brought silence and fear in the dark spirit , it was King Stone rushing towards the lake in furious anger which radiated strength and ferocity , as he ran the ground trembled and the evil liquid gathered its strength to meet him face to face; the King walked straight into the hissing and fighting lake as he lifted the boy out of the lake, its dark liquids tried to claim the King and his son as one but the King roared and the lake fell placid in shame and fear. The King walked out and lay the boy down on safe land; he would live once the liquid had left his body.

Rahul awoke in the hospital with his family around him... the episode of him drinking and falling into the lake was over but not forgotten by his family. There were days before he felt himself again and was ready and strong enough to leave the hospital. He did not want to stir yet more worry for anyone or bring more shame. The small pain that he felt inside him was gone but now there was nothing again and he knew it was worse than before, there was no remedy no cure and he had abused his body enough to find that out.

Megha had said many things before she told him that she could not be with him, she had said he needed to be alone to decide where he wanted to be and who he wanted to be. That she could not leave him trying to become someone he was never going to be...what did she know? What did she know about being alone...he had struggled enough his entire life trying to be someone and this was what he had done it for... for denial...had he not received it enough in his life? Was he that bad a person that he deserved no happiness...that the only thing he could ever feel was misery and guilt? So many times he had wondered if it were worth living this way and every single time he had told himself that there was a reason for him to be this way....good or bad.

He was different and he knew it. Why? Because he had to accomplish something the normal people could not accomplish due to things that hold them now, due to their limitations of being normal and happy with that. That's what he told himself. So many nights alone he had spent, even when with people because he knew he was wasting time in things that he did not need, nights alone and sleep less trying to understand what it was that he must do. What was his mission; Free Thought? Maybe it was that but some nights the struggle overcame the cause and left him paralyzed with guilt and tiredness and grief...it was too much for a single person to do...how could just he make a difference in the world so corrupt with content and so ignorant to see? He would have to be a genius, an affluent person or someone who the world looked up to...but that again would be fake; means to an end...he was familiar with that more than most. But by being someone significant he would be going against what he believed...that the only success that matters eventually is not measured by a pretty suit or a car, it is how much have you as a person contributed into solving the great question of life and death and aware have you been about your life and the millions of possibilities of every move that you make and if you can or cannot look above the cubicle of your work and see if the person across is happy or even try to connect with anyone around you....he felt nothing but he felt pain and sadness, the people he wanted to awake lacked empathy; only so much can be said about the shadows of the people that were existent anymore...the walkers had plagued the earth and the sloth had eaten through it the wings had sold their flight and become whores of the imbeciles spending the rest of their life trying to appeal to a mind inferior to theirs for wanting their money and their approval. It was pathetic and they knew it.

Finally a Flight

He had tried fighting the battle by staying under the shadows and showing the people that a greater knowledge will not be a burden but a priceless gift of awakening from a slumber so deep and consuming that they would have never realized they were alive.

He made his peace with all that had happened till now in an instant there was no more pain, no more anger, no more fear only the flame inside him licked him ; it was stronger than it had been for a long time.

His body felt weakness and his mind ached of all the stupidity he had done, he had drifted away from his resolve and his means of absolution, no more now…from the depths of the well of oblivion the boy with the broken wings screamed out for release and for the final time fought back from his grave to rise once again.

As he rose, Rahul knew that he no longer was the boy with the broken wings but there again were his wings spreading wide and strong, powerful beyond imagination and more magnificent than the shining sun itself.

He felt his ragged body once again come alive with the strength and life of the wings, he knew there was no longer a responsibility on him to make the world turn but there was a path for absolution and he was ready for what it brought to him, there was nothing to lose and as he started to rise above moving to face the great tree, finally his thoughts ran back to his family ; his father, his mother, his sister the only people who had seen him through to his every struggle...to Megha...her hair, her smile. He smiled knowing that he had perhaps made a difference in her life, that she would become someone who could think for herself.

He rose above the walkers and moved up the intricate branches and roots that blocked his way, above the strong trunk and the falling raining leaves he crossed it all rising above his own previous flight.

His wings pushed him forward tearing through the canopy of leaves and branches all trying to ebb away his momentum and throw him down but all in vain. He felt nothing as he moved through countless blockages and tunnels of obstacles keeping his mind fixed and his resolve steady, he pushed and fought his way so caught up shouting in rage that there was nothing to fight anymore.

He stood face to face with the great tree at last, above the canopy of leaves that he saw from below was a great trunk carved into which were a thousand faces. One of the faces spoke to him in a booming gaunt voice "how dare you defy us!!! Return back at once to the level you were born to!!!", another face spoke "I can see you are different...come closer...I want to be close to you" in a seductive tone, one face shouted "god will condemn you for this treason!!" Some faces shouted in languages he could not understand, some of the faces cried and the others laughed, some mouthed obscenities at him and the others tried to calm him down.

It was the voices of a thousand faces screaming and mixing

into each other creating chaos and nothing more. "This cannot be it" he thought as he saw the macabre sight of a thousand twisted faces now too busy shouting and abusing that they hardly noticed his presence.

"Silence!!" he shouted in a voice laced with command and anger.

"What are you?"He asked the thousand faces.

"We are the faces of humanity,
The rulers and masters of all
We control the petty working of some
Some we make them fall
We nurture the one who work
And ridicule the ones who can't
We give and take life
Simply as we want
We point fingers at sinners
Or whom we think are
Different or queer
In any way
We flood all with fear and spite
Simply because we care
We make sure the rich
Become more richer by day
And the poor
Well what can we say?
They die day by day
We mock the ones with faith
Like puppets we use them all
And blind them in every way
We are the ones who make battles start
And watch them become wars

We watch the illiterates control the earth
They lie standing tall
We are the society of thoughts
And the prison of minds
The keepers of sane and insane

We stand as old as time"

He looked at the faces as he laughed and cried at the same time and realized that the great evil he had battled against all his life was nothing more than a chimera of humanity.

"We see your confusion boy, and we know of your struggle to get here, you are neither the first nor the last to be different, how does that make you feel?" The ancient voice trailed away maliciously.

"Some of us here resent you, some of us sympathies with you, some of us even adore you but there remains one question. What now? This is where your journey led you to, you may have despised and fought against the branches and roots that clamped your feet to the ground but it was for your own good child! What could you hope to expect by rebelling against your keepers? We are necessary so that all of you may stay sane and keep functioning. There are darker sides of our under bellies that are present also there are platforms that radiate strength and compassion, we are everything that is good and bad in the world and all of us are equally necessary for all of you to exist. You fight against us because it is in your very nature and so you should, so the old roots do not get rusty and the old branches do not fall away, we are the constraints that will take you to your liberation child, to meet your purpose. Each person has a seed of destiny that they are born with and they can make the seed grow and enjoy its fruits or they can let it die, we give everyone to choose and decide their lives. We keep them oblivious of the bigger questions because if every mind was special then no mind is special, there always has to be one who breaches and finds the truth and the others catch up when they are ready to accept the truth; not everyone has wings like yours child."

"I have no spite against you Sirs and Madams, I know now the reason you exist. I want to know my mission; my purpose."

"Are you going to ask us what to do after you have fought against us for such a long time?" The voice laughed. Your great journey against conformity has led you to this?" A thousand voices piped into a macabre laughter. "We don't know your mission or purposes, we only know that the passage of time brings about people like you from time to time and sadly my child you are much ahead of you time, premature almost. You are an infant amidst a universe that is older than anything fathomable, wider than your wildest imagination and has mysteries that no one could ever understand. Grow in this universe and find your place. You were not meant to walk that I can see but you are yet a tiny speck completely insignificant and will always be so but your pursuit for knowledge will be possible as impossible and difficult it may be, it is possible."

"How do I grow?"

"You grow as you always have child, understand your insignificance and embrace it, adore it, you have to fly with it not despite it. The truth will find you once you are ready, till then you do as you are meant to do and you will fly as far as you want, these branches and roots will bother you never henceforth and though you may choose to walk remember where you want to grow. Do not worry about being a messiah and sharing what you know, you are required to feed the seed of your own destiny and the rest shall find it when they are ready."

He looked above and saw the tree expanding into the cosmos as his father had always told him, he belonged to the cosmos even if not on land and the boy was no longer sad or unhappy but a brimming confidence filled within him that his lonesome and tiring journey had brought him to the place he always wanted to be.

It was morning when Rahul woke up sitting on his bed watching the sun rise above in the window; he felt no gnawing of demons or urgency. He had slept well in the night as he wanted to give his body the rest it needed. He saw his hands and the scars that were etched into them. He could not remember being as unhappy as he had always been almost as if all that had never happened but felt sure about himself now. The fire was well alive inside him and though you could not see it but his wings embraced him stronger and purer than you could ever imagine.

Epilogue

Rahul quit his job as the manager of whatever company and traveled to different places in the world for three years; he came back and took up teaching. Megha kept writing for newspapers and magazines for some time but then later on started her own publishing house which publishes bi-monthly and soon became a respectable publishing house in the international market for publishing very strong material on cognitive development that the world needs to do. Mr. Trivedi left his job in the university many years after his last encounter with Megha and now is an active part of Megha's publishing house. Anagha and Candy joined an advertising firm and became senior partners there , Rohan joined his family business and brought forward commendable changes to the traditional frame, he wrote articles for Megha's magazine many times. King Stone and Lady River started an NGO titled 'Pathfinders' which bridged the poors to those who could help them, the Rain started her own online marketing company and later sold it for a serious amount of money.

All these characters and the real people behind them have perished with time and soon will be forgotten by the generation soon to follow them. Their ideals, their struggle all will be passed on as a gist of how they lived their lives. This fate awaits all of us and it is only a matter of time before the curtains fall on the small charade that we call life, really how much is a hundred years in a universe which is older than billions of years?

We may never know the truth about life but we cannot forget that it exists and no matter how much we have done know there is always more that can be done. Is it so different to live in day and night if the sun and moon both illuminate as one.

Megha opened the door and saw Rahul standing looking gaunt and his eyes as cold as ice staring into hers.

"Rahul...."

"You told me, either murderer or martyr...those are the options you gave me remember? "He whispered "well...I've made up my mind!" he sneered taking out a knife from behind.

Megha screamed and screamed as Rahul entered the house and tripped over the entrance door. Megha stared at him and started laughing as he stood as gawky as she remembered him to be. He stood up smiling picking the knife that had fallen away "like I could ever become a murderer."

They caught up on things over coffee and went out for a movie. "You could crash on the couch if you wanted" Megha said coyly.

Rahul smiled and they went inside the house and changed their clothes as it had begun to rain now.

Inside the house the old intimacy became alive in the dark and soon they were kissing and moved to the bedroom.

Rahul lit a cigarette after they had made love and stroked Megha's hair as she slept besides him.

"What did you do then Rahul?"

"I wrote."

"How many?"

"Three books."

Megha sat up looking at him, "I don't suppose you want to publish them."

Rahul laughed "I've spread them, like the one that brought you to me."

Megha sighed and smiled at him "get some rest you."

"The night is young Megha, and the wicked deserve no rest."

Author's Note

I hope you enjoyed reading the book; it's my first stab at book writing. As cynical as the characters might seem what they say and go through are real life situations and real life problems. The whole point of the book and I hope you already get it by now is for the reader, YOU to think beyond what you see, to think about and live life as a journey rather than an obligation or daily routine. It is Rahul's belief that our society can be better than what it is and the suffering he endures is his agony at his failure to make other people see it. Are we really so decadent that we must kill each other for land, for money? This truly cannot be it, that's what Rahul says. This cannot be the reason for evolution and our existence. As sceptical Rahul is about society he simply cannot accept it as it is and sees the norms of society as shackles that restraint most from even dreaming.

The poems, well all of them have been written by me in situations when I could find no escape other than writing down how I felt. There truly is a struggle behind them. I have imbibed them in the story line to bring about an inception of a thought that is not mutilated at birth by stigma and society.

Megha has been brought into the story to observe from an ordinary person's point of view the working of Rahul's thought process and titrate the thoughts to the real world scenario; are they feasible? Are they practical?

Even though one may say that Rahul ended up in the same place he started, anonymously placing his books in remote places; he has grown as a person, as all of us do. He is not an elite but rather an underdog.

So again,

 I am hoping that I have lit amber for you to catch fire.